Horse in a

D1650763

Patricia Leitch started riding when a friend persuaded her to go on a pony trekking holiday – and by the following summer she had her own Highland pony, Kirsty. She wrote her first book shortly after this and writing is now her full-time occupation, but she has also done all sorts of different jobs, including being a riding-school instructor, groom, teacher and librarian. She lives in Renfrewshire, Scotland, with a bearded collie called Meg.

More 'Jinny' books will be published in Armada

HORSE IN A MILLION

Patricia Leitch

AN ORIGINAL ARMADA

Horse in a Million was first published in Armada in 1980
by Fontana Paperbacks,
8 Grafton Street, London W1X 3LA.
This impression 1983

© Patricia Leitch 1980

Printed in Great Britain by
William Collins Sons & Co. Ltd., Glasgow.

CHAPTER ONE

Like leaves after an October gale, pages torn from Jinny
Manders' sketch pad littered her bedroom floor. Jinny knelt
in the middle of the room, her long red hair tenting her
sharp-featured face as she drew, considered, and then, with
a swift movement, tore off the page and sent it flying
through the air to join its fellows on the floor.

On each page, ponies and horses galloped and jumped,
their riders in hard hats and smart jodhpurs. Each drawing
was different—in some the ponies were fat, shaggy Thel-
wells; on some, elegant hacks and muscled hunters. Some
of the ponies scuttled between bending poles, or resisted at
the length of their reins while their riders tried to grab an
apple from a bucket with their teeth. The wise eyes of a
hunter looked out from a cluster of rosettes, and a show
pony with thoroughbred head and plaited mane was ridden
round a ring at an extended trot. In one of the drawings, the
horse was a chestnut Arab, leaping a spread jump of red and
white poles. The girl sitting, neat and tight, on its back had
long red hair flowing from beneath her hard hat.

Although all the drawings were different, the lettering
on each page never changed. Each page announced
FINMORY GYMKHANA in flaunting capitals.

Jinny tore the last page from her pad, stood up stretching
and stared down at her drawings.

"The pony ones are the best," she thought. "Then people
will know it isn't going to be a posh affair, just for fun."
And she picked out the best pony drawings and carried
them across to her bedroom window that looked out over
Finmory's garden, across fields, down to the sea.

Shantih and Bramble were grazing in the field at the foot
of the garden. Shantih belonged to Jinny. She was a pure-

bred, chestnut Arab, fleet and beautiful. Every line of her body, every silken hair of her mane and tail, her delicate ears, her dark lustrous eyes and her glistening white stockings, all sang of her breeding, of her quality, her perfection. Once she had been Yasmin, a circus killer horse, but Jinny had rescued her; fought for her life when she had been starving with an injured leg on the snow-covered Finmory moors, and gradually schooled her, until last autumn when Miss Tuke's Trekking Club had held a cross-country event and Jinny on Shantih had won a red rosette.

Bramble belonged to Miss Tuke. He was a black Highland with a heavy mane and long, thick tail. He regarded the world through his dense forelock, wise and considering —a fully paid-up member of the Highland ponies' trekking union. He knew his rights.

Shantih was the stars and the moon to Jinny, but Bramble was like a pair of old, comfortable slippers. Jinny thought of him as her own.

Two years ago, the Manders family had left the city suffocation of Stopton to come and live in grey stone Finmory House that stood in its own grounds between the sea and a wilderness of moorland.

In Stopton, Mr. Manders had been a probation officer, but since he had come to live in Scotland he had become a potter and had written a book about the appalling conditions in the Stopton slums. It had been published in January, linked with a T.V. programme, and now it was to come out in America and be translated into several languages. Her eyes watching Shantih, Jinny thought about the success of her father's book, how they had not had to worry about money since it had been published, how it meant that they might live at Finmory for ever.

Jinny switched back her mane of hair, spun round and grabbed her alarm clock. "It can't be right," she thought. "It can't be only ten past two." She shook it, but since its ticking made it unlikely that it had stopped, she could only hope that it had suddenly gone slow. The clock hands denied the possibility. It had never gone slow in its life. It was only, and exactly, ten past two.

"A whole half-hour before Sue can possibly get here," Jinny thought. Until Sue arrived she couldn't be certain that the Finmory gymkhana would actually happen. On the phone, Sue had been enthusiastic, but there was so much to arrange and maybe when Sue realised that it wasn't going to be the kind of organised gymkhana that her Pony Club ran she would lose interest, might even want to go home.

Last summer, Sue Horton, who was thirteen—the same age as Jinny—had spent the holidays camping with her parents in Finmory Bay. Sue had brought Pippen, her skewbald pony, and for the whole summer Jinny had had a friend to share her rides.

"If only Sue were back," Jinny had moaned, a week before her school broke up for the Easter holidays. "It's not nearly so much fun riding by myself."

"I thought this was to be the Easter of the Inverburgh Show?" Mike had asked. "Thought you'd be doing nothing but schooling Shantih, so you'd be brilliant to make up for last year's disaster."

"It is and I am," said Jinny severely. "But it would be more fun if Sue was here."

She ignored her brother's remark about last year's Inverburgh Show. He was right. It had been a disaster, an absolute disaster. "But it was all Clare Burnley's fault," Jinny thought. "Really I knew that Shantih wasn't ready for a show."

The Burnleys owned Craigvaar, a large detached house a few miles from Finmory. They didn't live there, but came up from England to spend their holidays in Scotland. At Easter, Clare brought two of her horses to Craigvaar. She took them both to the Inverburgh Show and always won all the cups.

"But of course it means absolutely nothing to me," she had told Jinny once. "I won my first cup in a Leading Rein class when I was three, and really I've just gone on from there. To tell you the truth, one has quite a shock when one doesn't win. One really takes it for granted, doesn't one?"

Hearing the sound of Clare Burnley's loud, self-confident voice in her ears made Jinny screw up her face with disgust. She had spent last Easter seeing Clare and her horses through a golden haze, until the haze was swept suddenly away and Jinny had realised what a fool she had been.

"If Sue were here," Jinny had said hurriedly to Mike, switching off from anything to do with the Burnleys, "we could have a gymkhana of our own. Sort of trial run for Inverburgh."

"Have it whether Sue is here or not," said Mike.

"You'd help me organise?"

Mike had grinned, pushing his fingers through his short, curly hair.

"Well, not really," he said. "There's the football team, and Mr. MacKenzie says I can drive his tractor."

"There you are," said Jinny. "That's why I need Sue."

"What's she doing?" asked Mrs. Manders.

"Don't know," said Jinny. "I'd a letter from her at Christmas and it's still my turn to write back."

"Perhaps she would like to come up for the holidays," Mrs. Manders had suggested. "Petra will be away on her music course most of the time. Be no problem."

"Oh yes," said Jinny, who had forgotten that her sister would be away. Petra was nearly sixteen years old, and, as far as Jinny could see, did nothing but bath herself and play the piano.

"Phone her," said Jinny's mother. "No harm in asking."

Jinny hesitated. "I wouldn't want to leave Shantih," she had said, "so I don't expect Sue would want to leave Pippen, and it would be far too expensive to bring him with her."

"She did last summer," said Mike.

"Behind their car."

"Galloping?"

Jinny had ignored him.

"Go on, phone," encouraged her mother. "For all you know, Sue may be longing to come back to Finmory. Do it now, then you'll know."

"Right," said Jinny. "Action this day."

10

She found Sue's phone number from one of her letters, looked up the correct dialling code and dialled. Holding the phone to her ear, she waited, listening to it ringing out, wondering who would answer. The phone rang on and on. Jinny's breathless expectancy changed to a dull certainty that there was no one at home.

"Count ten rings and then I'll put it down," she thought.

She had reached eight when someone lifted the receiver, and a breathless voice said, "Hullo," and added, "Sue Horton here."

"Nearly put it down," said Jinny, "I'd reached eight."

"What?" said Sue. "Pardon."

"I was counting to ten . . ."

"Jinny!" yelled Sue. "It is, isn't it? Jinny Manders!"

"Yes."

"You never wrote back. Not since Christmas."

"I meant to," said Jinny. "How are you?"

"Rotten," said Sue. "Pippen had a warble."

"A what?"

"Ghastly sort of maggot thing," explained Sue. "The fly lays its egg on the pony's leg. The pony licks its leg and swallows the egg. It hatches out and works its way right through to the pony's skin. A lump comes up on the pony's back, and once it's ripe, out pops the grub."

"Disgusting," said Jinny. "Poor old Pippen."

"Worse to follow," said Sue. "I didn't know about warbles, did I? So when I saw the lump on his back I thought it was only an insect bite, plonked his saddle on, and rode him at a rally. Killed the grub stone dead. It went rotten, and the vet has just been here gouging it out."

"Yuch."

"I know. Poultices for the next week and not to be ridden for three or four weeks. Just when the holidays are here. I could scream."

"Do," said Jinny. "You'll feel better."

Sue screamed.

"Well, in a way . . ." Jinny began, and was going to say it was a good thing that Pippen had been struck down, then changed her mind, realising that Sue couldn't be expected to see it quite like that.

"I'm phoning you to find out if you'd like to come and spend Easter with us. I said you wouldn't because of Pippen, but if your mother would look after him it would be a chance to come here." Jinny paused, half afraid that Sue would consider her heartless and yell that she couldn't possibly abandon Pippen in his warbled state.

"You could ride Bramble," offered Jinny, when Sue didn't speak.

"I'm struck dumb," said Sue. "It would be super. I'd love to come. I'd need to ask first, but I'm sure Mum would keep an eye on Pippen. She's quite keen on him now."

"I thought we might have a Finmory gymkhana," said Jinny.

"Yes! Oh yes!" enthused Sue.

Mrs. Manders came out to the phone, tapping her watch and mouthing, "What are you gossiping about?"

"Need to go," Jinny said to Sue. "Poverty-stricken parent grabbing phone."

"I'll ask," said Sue. "Whenever they get home."

"Phone me back."

"Will do, but I'm sure it will be O.K."

"Good," said Jinny. "Love to Pippen. Bye."

Sue had phoned back later in the evening to say that she could come, but her mother wanted to speak to Jinny's mother to make sure she was really wanted.

"I'll write. Tell you about the gymkhana," said Jinny, giving the phone to her mother who made "but of course we'd love to have her" noises to Mrs. Horton.

Jinny's school had broken up on the Wednesday and Sue was to arrive on the Friday. Jinny had been expecting to go with her father into Inverburgh to meet the train, but, to her dismay, the car had been full of a load of pots bound for Nell Storr's shop, where he sold his pottery.

"Sue will think it very odd if I don't come," Jinny had stated indignantly. "Asking her here, and only you to meet her."

12

"I'll explain," said Mr. Manders. "Can't be helped. Full load of goodies for the Easter tourists."

"Couldn't I hold them on my knee?"

"Sorry, the car's packed. I'll have Sue back here at the double."

Mr. Manders—balding, red-bearded, and wearing his potter's image of black jeans and pink smock—had driven off, leaving Jinny standing at the back door.

"Bit mean," she said aloud, feeling herself on the edge of umbrage. "Bet I could have fitted in somewhere."

"Don't sulk," Jinny told herself. "Don't spoil it. In two and a half hours Sue will be here." And the thought of the gymkhana blew up inside Jinny, filling her with excitement.

Dashing through the stone-floored kitchen, she leapt up the broad flight of stairs, ran along the long corridor and up the almost vertical stairs that led to her own room.

Jinny's bedroom was one large room, divided into two by an archway. One window looked out over Shantih's field to the sea. Jinny's bed was in this half, so she could sit up in bed and see Shantih first thing in the morning.

The window in the other half of her room looked out in the opposite direction, over the stretching moorland to the far mountains. One of the walls in this room was covered with Jinny's drawings and paintings. On the opposite side was the mysterious wall painting of the Red Horse. It had been there when the Manders had come to Finmory. Yellow-eyed, it charged from the wall, hooves plunging through a growth of white flowers.

Jinny had found some felt-tipped pens and, kneeling on the floor, started to draw posters for the gymkhana. She seemed to have been drawing for hours and yet, if the clock was right there was still over half an hour to wait until Sue arrived.

Jinny sat watching Shantih and Bramble nibbling each other's necks, and thought about mounted games. "Definitely bending," she decided. "And possibly musical poles."

A lean figure walked across the garden, towards the path that led to the sea. Shadowing his heels was Kelly,

13

a grey shaggy dog. It was Ken Dawson who lived with the Manders. He had followed them to Finmory from Stopton, where he had been on probation for an offence that he had had nothing to do with. Ken was eighteen, tall and lanky, with fair, shoulder-length hair. His rich parents sent him a cheque through their bank every month but refused to see him.

Last autumn, Ken had gone to Holland to work for a master potter, and Finmory had been lost without him. Jinny remembered the emptiness and the fear of the months when Ken had been away and she had thought that he would never come back. She shivered, perched on the sunlit windowsill. But it was over now. Past. Ken had come home to stay.

"Cross-country or show jumping?" Jinny wondered, scribbling the words on the back of a poster sketch. It would depend on Mr. MacKenzie—which field he let them use.

"Need to be one sort of showing class. Perhaps Best Turned Out Horse and Rider . . ."

Jinny heard the sound of the car. Sheets of paper flying from her, she sprang for the door. Tearing through the house, she was just in time to reach the front door as the car drew up. Sue flung the car door open and came running towards Jinny.

"Wait till you see what I've got," she cried.

"What?"

"Can't tell you. Must show you," said Sue. Her wide, generous mouth was set in a huge grin; her hazel eyes twinkled with laughter as she teased Jinny.

"Lovely to see you," said Mrs. Manders, coming out to greet Sue. "What kind of journey did you have?"

"Boring," said Sue. "Couldn't get here quickly enough. It is very, very kind of you to invite me," she added, being polite but all the time laughing at Jinny.

"We're so glad you could come," said Petra, shaking hands. "Jinny's got this idea about holding a gymkhana. Be warned."

"I know," said Sue. "I think it's a smashing idea, and

14

wait till you see what I've got for it. Dad sent it. I think he's so pleased not to have me groaning around the house, going on about Pippen's warble. Even the thought makes him sick."

Mr. Manders brought Sue's case into the hall.

"It's in there," Sue said. "Do you mind if I open it here? Mum would, but she'll never know and I must let Jinny see it at once."

Jinny watched as Sue crouched down and unlocked her case. "Something for the gymkhana," she thought. "Something that Mr. Horton has given us." Jinny held her breath. Stopped herself imagining that it could possibly be . . .

"A cup," cried Sue, holding aloft a silver cup. "For Finmory's gymkhana."

Jinny let out her breath in a long gasp of total admiration. She stared, spellbound, at the cup. It wasn't a mean, goose-eggcup size, but satisfyingly big, with silver handles on either side so that when you cantered your winning round you could hold it up above your head.

"Actually, it's not new," Sue admitted. "Dad won it years ago. But you'd never know. There's nothing on it, only the place where he was meant to have it engraved but never got round to it. It's to be for the best horse or pony. The one who wins the most points. Games, showing and jumping. Well, say something. Don't just stand there."

"She can't," laughed Mrs. Manders.

"How did you know?" demanded Petra. "Only last night she was going on at us all, about how we must be the only family in the world who had never won a cup. How all other families had rows of silver cups."

Jinny hardly heard her mother or her sister. Beneath her she felt the smooth beat of Shantih's galloping hooves, in front of her reached Shantih's arched neck and delicate head. The applause echoed in Jinny's ears as she rode. In one hand she held Shantih's reins, and in the other she held Sue's cup above her head.

"A cup!" she said at last. "A real cup for Finmory's gymkhana!"

CHAPTER TWO

"I thought we'd ask Miss Tuke to be the judge," said Jinny to Sue.

"Won't she be trekking?"

"Saturday should be O.K. for her. That's the day the trekkers change over. I phoned her up about the gymkhana and she more or less agreed. I thought we could ride over tomorrow and ask her properly."

Sue was sleeping on the camp bed in Jinny's room. Mrs. Manders had said it was ridiculous when there were so many empty bedrooms in Finmory, but Sue had insisted that she would much rather share with Jinny so they could chat. They had gone to bed at about ten, now it was half-past twelve and they were still chatting.

"And on our way there, we'll make sure that Mr. MacKenzie hasn't changed his mind about letting us have his field," said Jinny.

Mr. MacKenzie's farm was the only other building close to Finmory, and Jinny knew the old farmer well.

"Imagine them all turning up, and Mr. MacKenzie barring the way with a pitchfork in his hand."

"We'd have to hold it on the shore," said Jinny, and saw, for a moment, ponies racing across the sands or a cross-country course set out between the boulders. "But he won't. He likes Miss Tuke."

Jinny heard her parents' bedroom door open, her father's footsteps marching down the landing.

"Get to sleep," he shouted up at them from the foot of Jinny's stairs. "It's long past midnight."

"We are asleep," Jinny yelled back.

"Good," said her father, and pounded back to bed.

Next day was blue sky and high, wind-blown clouds, flying light and shade chasing over the moors.

16

Immediately after breakfast, Sue and Jinny caught Shantih and Bramble and gave them a thorough grooming, so they would pass Miss Tuke's eagle scrutiny.

When they had saddled up and were ready to go, Jinny went back into the house to let her mother know that they were away. Ken was standing by the window, drinking his own brew of herb tea. He never ate or drank anything that came from an animal.

"Going to pot?" Jinny asked him.

"I am," said Ken.

"We're riding to Miss Tuke's."

"And what a morning for it," said Ken. "Use your ears. Smell it in. Feel how your eyes carry it all into your head. Hear the silence. Hear the roar of constant re-creation. The lion's roar. The NOW."

"To ask her," continued Jinny, "if she'll come and judge at our gymkhana."

Ken groaned. "What a nonsense," he said mildly. "Judging! Phawgh, I spit it from my mouth."

"I expect," said Jinny, "Miss Tuke will present the cup." She didn't add "to me", but she knew Ken knew that was what she was thinking.

"Why ever do you want to tie tin cups on to yourself?"

"It means you're a winner," said Jinny, knowing she was wasting her time arguing with Ken.

"Winner?" mocked Ken. "There's nothing to win. We all have everything."

"It means you are the BEST and everyone else knows you are the BEST."

"Listen to how you weave yourself into a web of wanting," said Ken, looking straight at Jinny.

"Right," said Jinny. "I want to win that cup. I do. I don't care what you say. I think it's dreadful the way this family have never won anything. All other families have cups they've won, and I'm going to win it. Sue has won lots of cups."

Ken shrugged, rinsed out his cup at the sink, holding it under the running tap water and drying it with care before he hung it from its hook.

"Do what you must do," he said to Jinny.

"Smug," said Jinny, as he went off to the pottery, but the word wouldn't stick because he wasn't.

"Take care," said her mother, when Jinny found her.

"As always," said Jinny.

"And the milk can," reminded her mother.

"As always," said Jinny.

Bramble trotted beside Shantih as the two girls rode down the path to Mr. MacKenzie's farm.

"It is super being back," said Sue, gazing about her as she rode. "We don't exactly live in town, some people call it the country, but it's not like this. All this space and freedom."

Glancing at the moorland stretching to the mauve-blue mountains, and down to where the cliffs of Finmory Bay were jet against the sea dazzle, Jinny knew exactly what Sue meant, but this morning her mind was on other things.

"I'll bet your family have won lots of cups," she asked, checking up in case she was wrong.

"A few," admitted Sue. "Pippen has won some at Pony Club things."

"How many?" demanded Jinny, wanting facts.

"Five. Of course, I only kept them for a year, but they give you a little one with your name and the date on it and that is yours to keep. Dad has several he's won for his bowling, and Mummy has two that she won years ago for dog training."

"I knew I was right. Proper families all have cups."

"All they are is a nuisance to dust."

"Because you've won them," said Jinny. "It is quite utterly different when you've never won one."

Mr. MacKenzie, hearing the sound of hooves in his yard, came out of the byre.

"It's yourself returned," he said to Sue.

"It is."

"And wise you were to go south for the winter. Only those with the screws a wee bit loose would be staying here for the snows to catch them."

"My screws must be rattling," declared Sue. "I'd stay here all the time if I could."

"You'd think, to be looking at you, that you'd have more sense. Now you'll be here for the milk," he said to Jinny, taking the milk can from her, clattering its lid and making Shantih dance sideways in a flurry of mane and tail.

"Mike will collect it," said Jinny. "We're riding over to Miss Tuke's to see if she'll judge at our gymkhana next Saturday. In your field?"

"I was not forgetting it. You can be having the flat field for the day. It's dry enough now. You'll not be doing much damage to it."

"Good," said Jinny thankfully. "Are you coming to spectate?"

"If you give me your word on it that Miss Tuke will be for the jumping, I'll be there."

"She might be," said Jinny, thinking that she couldn't imagine Miss Tuke show jumping.

"I saw her once, and the old horse she was on went as neat as sixpence right to the jump. To the very jump he went, put his front feet together and stopped to say his prayers. But Miss Tuke was not for the stopping, on she went and took the jump by herself and to hell with the horse."

The old farmer paused, and spat reflectively into the midden.

"And when she got herself up, was there not a hole in the ground as if a bomb had hit it. Oh, I'll be there if you can promise me the likes of that again."

"I'll ask Miss Tuke," promised Jinny.

"She'll be remembering it fine. They'd to move the jump away from the crater before the show could go on. Be asking her yourself," said Mr. MacKenzie.

"Don't worry, we will," Jinny assured him. "And it is all right about the field?" she called after him as he turned into the byre.

"Aye, but mind now, I'm expecting to see Miss Tuke in action."

"Do my best, but I think she'll be judging," Jinny promised, as she and Sue rode out of the yard.

"He is in a good mood," said Sue, remembering Mr. MacKenzie from the summer.

"I think it's the new grandson. He was only three months old when I saw him, but if you'd put a pipe in his mouth and a cap on his head you'd have sworn it was Mr. MacKenzie."

They trotted on until they came to the first of the forestry roads that led to Miss Tuke's. Shantih, feeling the softer ground beneath her hooves, clinked her bit and with a half-rear suggested they gallop.

"O.K.?" Jinny called back over her shoulder, but already Shantih was away.

For minutes, Jinny was lost in a blur of speed. Shantih's effortless stride was so smooth that Jinny hardly moved in the saddle as Shantih stretched low to the ground, her ears laid back, her nostrils blood-red pits. Bramble's heavy hoofbeats drummed behind them.

Jinny waited until Shantih's first burst of speed had worn itself out, then she sat down in the saddle and, playing with the bit, speaking gently to her horse, gradually settled her into a collected canter. Sue drew level with them, tugging valiantly at Bramble's mouth.

"He's like a train," Sue yelled, as Bramble carried her past Jinny.

"Once you're in front he'll stop pulling," Jinny told her, as Bramble surged ahead, and his storming speed steadied into a bustling but controllable gallop.

"I haven't galloped like this since I was here," Sue gasped, when at last a closed forestry gate made them stop. "Miss Morris would have heart failure. Only the Orange Ride is allowed to canter. We're in it, but the minute Pippen begins cantering she's squeaking at us to steady up."

"Can't you gallop when you're riding by yourself?"

"There really isn't anywhere," stated Sue. "You don't know how lucky you are."

"I do. I used to live in Stopton. You couldn't even keep a pony in Stopton."

"I do think Shantih has improved," Sue said, as they rode on. "Or you have."

"Bit of both," Jinny said, clapping Shantih's hard shoulder.

"She just took off with you before, but she was cantering beautifully for you there."

"I've been schooling her like anything," admitted Jinny. "I've entered her for the Inverburgh Show. Not that I expect to win anything. I only want her to behave herself. It's the Saturday after our gymkhana."

"Can I take Bramble?"

" 'Course," said Jinny. "You can enter on the field. Actually, it's mostly agriculture, sheep and cows and tractors, but there are a few horsy things. Open Jumping classes, open to anyone on anything. There was a boy last year on a Fell pony. He only had one refusal, but Clare Burnley won it on her fancy showjumper." Jinny snorted with disgust at the thought.

As they drew closer to Miss Tuke's, Bramble's head went up, he whinnied with excitement and made sudden, excited dashes forward.

"He always knows," said Jinny. "Wait till you get nearer—you won't be able to hear yourself think."

When Bramble reached the hoof-rutted path that led to Miss Tuke's trekking centre, he threw up his head, almost banging Sue on the nose, and gave vent to a clarion whinny. Again and again, completely ignoring Sue's correct aids, he stopped and screamed to his fellow Highlands.

Miss Tuke was standing in the yard, a muddle of rope halters in her hands.

"Jolly glad to see you," she cried, which Jinny took to be an excellent omen. "Was going to have to do the whole job myself. Taken me three trips at least. Been the whole blooming day at it, but now that you've turned up we'll do it in a oner."

"Do what?" Jinny asked suspiciously. "We've come to

21

see you about our gymkhana." But Miss Tuke wasn't paying any attention to her.

"You're the Horton girl, aren't you?" she was saying to Sue. "Don't tell me. Never forget a name. Sue. Sue Horton. Your old man took rather a header. Never forget a trekker. How is he? Recovered?"

"Totally. Back to his bowling."

"Best thing," said Miss Tuke. "Hadn't got the makings. No stamina. Now, take a couple of halters each. Leaves three for me. Should manage. I'll ride Donald—solid as a rock."

"What are we going to do?" Jinny almost shouted.

"Bring them down from the hill. Don't need them for the trekking yet, but with the tinks arriving I'm taking no chances. The meat men are paying a fortune for horse flesh. Putting temptation in the tinkers' way, leaving them up there. Get the little blighters down where I can keep an eye on them." And giving Jinny and Sue two rope halters each, Miss Tuke marched off to the stables.

"The winter's been too much for her," Jinny whispered. "Gone bonkers!"

"Dangerous," giggled Sue. "Better play it her way."

Miss Tuke came back from the stables, leading a miniature carthorse. She had a bucket of pony nuts hanging over her arm and three halters tied round her like climbers' ropes. Clanking the bucket against the bay pony's side, she heaved herself into the saddle.

"Trek forward," she called, rousing Sue and Jinny to follow her.

"We've been press trekked," said Sue, forcing the reluctant Bramble out of the yard.

"But what are we going to do?" demanded Jinny, trotting Shantih alongside Miss Tuke.

The bay Highland swished his tail and snapped at Shantih.

"Donald!" roared Miss Tuke in thunderous tones. "Of course, he's used to being in front," she added to Jinny. "Not accustomed to being charged from behind."

"Where are we going?"

"Subnormal?" asked Miss Tuke. "All the brain bashing you've had, falling off that mad mare."

"Where . . .?"

"Up the hill, to bring the rest of my ponies down to the paddock. Be heels and teeth, but we'll manage."

"How far?"

Miss Tuke gestured vaguely towards the skyline and the mountains. Jinny groaned. Since they had come to ask Miss Tuke to judge for them, they couldn't very well refuse to help her.

First they followed the track of trekking ponies' hoof-prints between high avenues of pine trees, then they went through a forestry gate which they left open.

"Less hassle on our way back," Miss Tuke said. "I'll pop back and shut it this evening."

They rode on along the forestry track until Miss Tuke opened a gate that led on to the steep hillside.

"Nearly there." Miss Tuke pointed to a wire fence about halfway up the hillside. "Look out for them there."

"Won't they be difficult to catch?" Sue asked.

"Not a bit of it. They see me as meals on hooves."

There was a shrill neighing, a stampede of hooves, and a mob of Highlands came careering down the hill. At the wire fence they broke to left and right, squealing and kicking as they plunged and bucked.

"I bet they haven't had a halter near them since the trekking finished last year," Jinny said, low-voiced, to Sue.

"Whoa the ponies! Steady the little horses! Whoa now," Miss Tuke called in calming tones as they climbed towards the fence, but her voice only seemed to make the ponies more excited.

"They know the bucket," she said. "Be fun and games when they realise what's what."

They rode alongside the fence, the Highlands racing beside them, until they came to a gate.

"Now I'll go in," announced Miss Tuke, in the manner of a lion tamer about to enter a lion's cage. "Off you get and I'll hand them out to you one by one."

Grasping the bucket in one hand and shouting threats

23

and curses at the top of her voice, Miss Tuke thrust her way into the mass of Highlands.

"Sunk without trace," said Jinny, as she vanished from sight.

"We should have asked her about being the judge first," said Sue.

"No point now she's trampled to death."

In minutes Miss Tuke had re-emerged, towing a dun Highland behind her.

Jinny gave Shantih to Sue, who was already holding Donald, and went to take the pony from Miss Tuke.

"Tie a knot in the halters," she told Jinny. "Don't want them strangling themselves," and Miss Tuke dived back into the mass of ponies, who were all fighting to grab their share from the bucket.

In no time the bucket was empty, and all seven Highlands were haltered and on the other side of the gate.

"Bingo," exclaimed Miss Tuke, when she rejoined them. "Now, let's sort them out."

With a threat here and a yank on a halter rope there, Miss Tuke divided up the Highlands.

"Get back on your ponies," Miss Tuke said to the girls, "and I'll hand the ropes up to you."

She stared disapprovingly as Jinny hopped alongside the excited Shantih, trying to control her until she could spring on to her.

"Stand at peace, you crazy woman, you," bellowed Miss Tuke, losing her patience.

Shantih sprang to attention, the tips of her ears meeting in surprise and giving Jinny the chance to spring into the saddle.

Miss Tuke, controlling the ponies with one hand, somehow managed to pass halter ropes up to Jinny and Sue. Jinny found herself in charge of two dun ponies. Sue had a grey and a bay; Miss Tuke, two bays and a steel grey.

"Keep behind me," warned Miss Tuke, as she struggled back on to Donald. "Let them know who's boss."

"But I'm not," gasped Sue, as Bramble lashed out at the

grey, and the bay pony flung itself back to the full length of the halter rope.

"Off we go," shouted Miss Tuke, ignoring Sue's plight and starting to walk on downhill, coping somehow with three Highlands, Donald and the empty bucket.

It was easier once they were moving. Copying Miss Tuke, Jinny yanked at the Highlands' ropes, keeping their heads beside Shantih's shoulder.

"Shout at them," she told Sue, whose bay Highland was going backwards in an attempt to avoid Bramble's heels.

They were halfway down the hillside, and Jinny was just beginning to think it possible that they might reach the forestry track without some of the Highlands breaking loose, when, springing from nowhere, two brindled lurchers came racing across the moor towards them.

"Hounds of the Baskervilles," said Sue in despair.

"Hang on," yelled Miss Tuke, as the dogs, snapping and growling, sprang at the ponies' heels. "I'll chuck the bucket at them."

Jinny tightened her grip on her Highlands' ropes and dug her knees into her saddle.

"Get away with you," yelled Miss Tuke, and aimed her bucket.

Jinny heard the bucket crash to the ground, and Sue scream as Bramble charged off down the hillside in terror, the two Highlands plunging about him. She caught a glimpse of one of the lurchers leaping at Shantih, felt Shantih lash out, then explode beneath her as she reared up away from the dog.

"Steady! Steady!" yelled Jinny, as she felt the halter ropes burning through her hands. Trying to hold on to the Highlands, Jinny had dropped her own reins and Shantih, feeling herself free, put in one huge, starfish buck, then took off over the moor. Jinny could do nothing but try to hang on to the Highlands and stay on top of Shantih.

"Whoa! Whoa!" she cried desperately, as she tried to fumble for her reins and turn Shantih uphill.

The grey pony that Sue had been leading galloped past

25

them, its long halter rope dragging about its legs. Jinny glanced back, trying to see what was happening to Sue. In that instant, something made Shantih shy violently and Jinny was pitched out of the saddle, to fall into a confused mass of legs and hooves that for a second were plunging dangerously close to her face and, in the next, were galloping over the hill away from her.

Visions of broken legs caught in ropes or reins flashed through Jinny's mind as she struggled to her feet. A piercing whistle rang out over the hillside and Jinny knew why Shantih had shied.

A scarecrow man wearing a greasy, navy-blue suit with a scarf tied at his neck and a checked cap set on the back of his head, was standing close to Jinny. He glanced down at her, his dark eyes hard and glittering in his swarthy, unshaved face. The lurchers had left the ponies and were slinking unwillingly towards him.

Miss Tuke, shouting at the pitch of her lungs, still well in control of her three Highlands, came, mighty as a battalion of horse, trotting towards them.

"Get off this hill," she was roaring. "Get off my land."

The man's gaze flickered over her. He turned without hurrying and began to make his way back up the hill. From somewhere out of the bracken, a boy of about eight or nine, smear-faced, in torn jeans and a man's jacket, joined the lurchers and ran after him.

"You're here on Alec McGowan's farm and you'll stay on his land, or I'll have the police to you. Stay off my hill!"

Neither the man nor the boy glanced back. They reached the fence, ducked between the wire strands while the lurchers cleared it in an effortless, roe-deer leap, and in minutes they had vanished from sight round the hillside.

Jinny, who had been watching, mesmerised, came back to the reality of loose ponies and Shantih grazing with her leg through her reins—her only pair of reins.

"That's it started," blazed Miss Tuke. "They'll be round the house at all hours of the day and night. Picking up anything they can find. Nothing safe until we get rid of them. Why Alec McGowan lets them camp on his land I do not know. And I suppose this means I'll need to get another bucketful of nuts."

It took them nearly three hours to catch the Highlands. The grey pony Sue had been leading refused to come near them and, in the end, they had to drive it loose into Miss Tuke's yard.

"There," exclaimed Miss Tuke, when at last all seven ponies had been turned out into the paddock that stretched up into the hills from her yard. "Can keep an eye on them there."

"Pretty long eye," said Jinny, watching the ponies hightailing it up the hillside with the other Highlands who had already been in the field and had come down to investigate the intruders. "They'll be out of sight in a moment."

"Be down for nuts," said Miss Tuke. "I'm using some of the others for trekking. They'll all be together. Out on that mountaintop I had to make a safari to check up on them. Now, shove your gees into a box and we'll have some food ourselves."

Seated in Miss Tuke's study, over egg and chips followed by apple pie, they discussed the gymkhana. Miss Tuke had taken Jinny's phone call seriously and had been organising things from her end.

"All fixed up," she said. "Only too pleased to judge. Been in touch with the other members of the Trekking Club. Think they're all coming. Sara on Pym, Moira on Snuff and I'm providing Highlands for the others. I've two trekkers arriving today for a fortnight's trekking. Say they're experienced, which could mean Badminton or able to post. I'll bring them over with us. We'll all ride over. Grand trek! They'll love it and I'll survive."

Jinny sat listening, fascinated by Miss Tuke's organisation. Until now, the gymkhana had only really existed in Jinny's dreams, but Miss Tuke had pinned it out in reality.

"Now, let's get the classes sorted out. I thought one for Best Turned Out Horse and Rider—gives everyone a chance—and Best Suited Horse and Rider, for a giggle. Three jumping classes – Mini, Midi, Maxi," said Miss Tuke, writing the classes down as she spoke. "Mixture of walls and

27

jumps? See what there is. Three games—don't want to drag it out. Musical poles? Bending? I've got poles. And a potato race?"

Jinny and Sue nodded in silent agreement.

"How's the publicity going?" Miss Tuke asked, as she came out into the yard with them.

"I've more or less decided on the poster," said Jinny.

"Cow's tail!" exclaimed Miss Tuke. "Get it into the village shop at once. We want a few spectators."

"Monday," promised Jinny.

"Who is in the Trekking Club?" Sue asked, as they rode home.

"Three Hay boys and three ladies who ride Miss Tuke's Highlands. And Sara and Moira, who have their own ponies."

"Eight," said Sue. "And two trekkers. You and me—that's twelve. Not bad, if they all go in for every class."

Jinny gulped and nodded, seeing Mr. MacKenzie's field overflowing with Highlands.

"Watch out," Sue mouthed. "On your right. Under the trees. The tinkers."

Catching the fear in Sue's voice, Jinny searched the dark shadows of the pines. Standing so still that they seemed to be growing out of the ground, were the two tinkers they had seen at Miss Tuke's. The two lurchers lay at the man's feet, heads on outstretched paws, ears alert.

As Sue and Jinny rode towards them, neither the man nor the boy moved. They made no sign that they had seen either the girls or their ponies.

"Nice day," said Jinny, but her voice sounded high and strained; her smile felt pinned on to her mouth.

The man's black eyes stared through her, making her almost unsure whether she had spoken or not. From his hand dangled four dead rabbits.

"Gosh," said Sue, when they were past. "I see what Miss Tuke means. I wouldn't want them prowling about my house at night."

Jinny didn't reply. She didn't really know what she felt about the tinkers. She wasn't furious with them the way

28

Miss Tuke was, and she wasn't afraid of them like Sue. "Least they're not plastic," she thought, and for a moment Jinny saw herself riding with them, travelling on.

"Let's trot," said Sue, kicking Bramble.

Jinny looked back. The man had turned and was watching them. His eyes in the shadow of the trees were as lustrous as Shantih's, yet they had a cruel glitter that made Jinny shiver.

"Come on," said Sue impatiently. "We want to get the poster done tonight."

"We can put in about the cup," said Jinny, touching Shantih into a trot, and instantly her head was full of nothing but gymkhana plans.

CHAPTER THREE

First thing on Monday morning, Jinny and Sue rode into Glenbost with the gymkhana poster. Sue held Shantih while Jinny took the poster into Mrs. Simpson's sell-everything shop.

"Well?" said Mrs. Simpson, regarding Jinny without enthusiasm. "It's yourself is after the worm this morning."

She was standing behind her counter, holding a long-handled feather duster which she flicked randomly over cheese and wellingtons, chocolate biscuits, vegetables and tins of paint.

"We're holding a gymkhana at Finmory," Jinny explained.

"And what sort of thing would that be?" interrupted Mrs. Simpson, stopping in mid flick, feather duster motionless.

"A gymkhana," repeated Jinny. "You know. Competitions for ponies. Jumping and racing. It's all on the poster."

Jinny ducked under the feather duster and spread the poster out on the counter.

Mrs. Simpson looked at the decoration of galloping ponies without a sign of interest. She studied the events and read the gold lettering that announced the cup, without a shade of expression showing on her face.

"The cup," said Jinny, pointing. "There's a cup for the best horse and rider."

Mrs. Simpson's duster did a quick sortie over a cluster of buckets that hung from the ceiling. "It'll be thirty pence," she said, "for the week."

"Thirty pence?"

"That's what I'm charging. You'll be wanting it in my window, I'm thinking, and thirty pence it will cost you, paid in advance."

"Well, I do. That's what we brought it for, so everyone will see it and come. It says—look—spectators welcome."

"Thirty pence," repeated Mrs. Simpson.

Jinny, who hadn't expected to pay anything, had to go out to borrow the money from Sue.

"I think I've got fifty pence in my pocket," said Sue. "Here, take your idiot until I prise it out."

Shantih, impatient at the delay, was tiptupping about, head raised, nostrils flared, tail kinked over her back. As always, Jinny could only think how beautiful she looked when she was excited like this.

"Shall we go down on to the beach afterwards and school?" Sue asked, giving Jinny the money, so that Jinny knew Sue saw Shantih as wild and untrained, not free and romantic as Jinny saw her.

But it was different now, Jinny thought. Shantih wasn't wild and uncontrollable the way she had been a year ago, and Jinny looked back with a self-satisfied, well-done-Jinny-Manders glow, over all the schooling she had done during the past weeks.

"Right," said Jinny. "I'll just pay Mrs. Scrooge, then we can go home by the shore and school on the sands."

Mrs. Simpson took the fifty pence, gave Jinny her change, tore a strip of Sellotape from the roll on her counter and, leaning across battlements of toilet rolls, sacks of sugar and a mound of butter, stuck the poster in the window.

"It's squint," said Jinny.

Mrs. Simpson snorted, feather duster at the ready.

"It is," said Jinny. "Honestly."

Grudgingly, Mrs. Simpson tore off another scrap of Sellotape and straightened the poster.

"You will come, won't you?" said Jinny.

"It's that man MacKenzie should be having his head examined, encouraging you with such goings on," she said, giving high-speed, furious flicks at the side of bacon sitting on the slicing machine.

"Bye," said Jinny.

"Looks smashing," said Sue, as they examined the poster from outside.

"Super," agreed Jinny. "You can see the bit about the cup from here."

"Do you think there is anyone else with a pony who might see it and come?"

"No," said Jinny. "Not a chance. I'd know about them if there was anyone. Still, I expect lots of children will come to watch."

They rode down to the shore, clattering over the bank of sea-smooth pebbles and then on down to the sands. The tide was out and a glimmering expanse of sand stretched before them.

Jinny trotted Shantih in wide circles at a sitting trot. She rode with long reins, feeling her horse relax. Then, gradually, she gathered Shantih together, asking her to balance herself, take more of her weight on her quarters, lift her head, lighten her forehand. They circled at a collected trot, then, when Jinny was satisfied that Shantih was really using herself, she touched her on with her leg and they were cantering. Not the mad surging burst of speed that had been so typical of Shantih a few months ago, but a smooth, easy change into a balanced canter.

"Good," Jinny whispered. "Good. Well done."

As they cantered round, Jinny felt her mouth spreading into a grin of delight. She turned Shantih to make a figure eight, and realised that Sue had stopped schooling and was watching them.

"Easy now, easy," Jinny murmured.

At the centre of the figure eight, Shantih changed legs with a perfect flying change. Jinny let out a long sigh of satisfaction. She was still teaching Shantih to change leg without breaking into a trot, and today had been the smoothest change she had managed.

"You have improved," said Sue, when Jinny slowed Shantih down and walked towards her. "Wish I had Pippen here. We could have a dressage comp."

"Go on," said Jinny, remembering how well-schooled Pippen had been. "You could have given us a demonstration ride. Shall we jump?"

"Where?"

"Mr. MacKenzie's field. It won't be cheating because we'll be changing all the jumps before the gymkhana."

"O.K.," said Sue, and they rode to Mr. MacKenzie's field, the only flattish field for miles around.

There were six jumps made from a collection of poles, old deck chairs, rusty oil cans and rotten straw bales.

"Have you been jumping those?" asked Sue suspiciously. "They're far higher than you used to jump."

"Well, Shantih is better now," said Jinny. "She understands what it's all about. Shall I jump first? And then I think we'd better put them down a bit for Bramble."

"Proceed," said Sue. "I am ready to be impressed."

"Never know," said Jinny. "Perhaps she won't jump at all today."

But she knew it wasn't likely. Already Shantih's ears were pricked and her eyes alight at the sight of the jumps.

Jinny gathered up her reins, cantered a circle, and, still moving at a collected canter, rode at the first jump. Shantih approached it steadily, calmly judging her take-off, and soared over it in a perfect arc. Hardly increasing her speed, she cantered on to the next jump and leapt sweetly over it, her forelegs tucked close to her body.

Jinny turned her and they cantered up the other side of the field, taking the jumps with the same effortless ease. Down the centre of the field they went, Jinny easing her fingers on the reins and allowing Shantih to increase her speed so that they were galloping towards the spread jump in the middle of the field. With a gay whisk of her tail, Shantih cleared it and went galloping on until Jinny asked her to canter.

"Stun," announced Sue, as Jinny walked Shantih calmly back towards her. "I'm into stun."

"She has improved," agreed Jinny, trying to keep her grin under control as she clapped Shantih's sleek neck.

"Improved! She's not the same horse. That's what it is. You've sold that mad crazy horse you had in the summer and bought this one from Caroline Bradley."

"Huh," said Jinny. "I might have known you'd spot the difference."

"How did you do it?" demanded Sue.

"Worked," stated Jinny. "Well, I thought hard about it. I knew she could jump because of jumping Mr. Mac-Kenzie's gate and an enormous jump over a waterfall, so really all I had to do was calm her down between jumps. I made the jumps tiny and schooled her in a circle over them till she was hardly noticing them. It was just like trotting in a circle. Then I made the circle bigger and sort of sneaked up the height on her."

"Child's play," said Sue, mocking. "Anyone could have done it."

"There were moments," admitted Jinny. "She went bonkers one night. Crashed through them all without jumping at all and took off with me. We finished up on the shore going straight for the sea, and when we reached the water she tipped me off and galloped back to Finmory without me. Didn't you?"

Shantih ignored her, pawing the ground with an elegant foreleg. Such things were in her past, if they had happened at all.

"Let me have a go," said Sue.

"I'd better take the bars off the spread," said Jinny, jumping to the ground. "And I'll squash down some of the others."

When Jinny had made the jumps into more Bramble-sized obstacles, Sue took him round. They had four refusals at the first jump and then Bramble realised that Sue really meant what she said. Head down, he charged round the jumps, getting right in under them before he shot vertically into the air. At the spread in the middle of the field he stopped dead, slipped his shoulder and deposited Sue, head first, into the jump.

"If he does that on Saturday, Mr. MacKenzie won't need Miss Tuke—I'll do instead," said Sue, as she remounted.

"Now get on with you," she shouted, and rode at the jump again.

Her heels kicking tightly into Bramble's hairy sides, Sue drove the pony over the jump.

"You should see his expression," said Jinny. "He is not happy."

"Happy!" exclaimed Sue. "I'll happy him. He's like a flying bedstead compared to Pippen."

"Don't," cried Jinny in horror. "Don't let him hear you saying things like that about him."

"That is nothing to what I shall be saying about him before Saturday," threatened Sue.

They rode back to Finmory, reins loose, feet free from their stirrups, the spring air warm about them.

"Will you have it engraved now?" Sue asked.

"Engraved?" asked Jinny, puzzled. Then she knew what Sue meant. "Don't be daft. Anyone might win it."

"Handful of trekking ponies and me on Bramble? You're bound to win the cup."

"I'm not," denied Jinny, feeling herself blush. "Sara's pretty good—and Moira."

"Not as good as Shantih," teased Sue.

"Well, nearly," said Jinny. "Better at games, I should think. Much better."

"You don't really think that."

"Let's canter," yelled Jinny, and before Sue had time to collect herself, Shantih and Jinny were galloping up the path to Finmory.

Giggling, Jinny looked back over her shoulder at Sue bumping up and down on Bramble. "That'll teach her to think I'm sure I'll win the cup," thought Jinny, as she urged Shantih on. "But you do," said the voice inside her head. "You're sure you'll win it."

"Rubbish," replied Jinny, forcing Shantih to go faster.

They spent the rest of the week preparing for Saturday. Mrs. Manders agreed to sell lemonade, biscuits and rolls on the field. Petra had left for her music course, but Mr. Manders, Mike and Ken all agreed to be stewards.

"You see, we won't be free to help," Jinny explained to them. "Sue and I are riding. But we'll make out score sheets for you and it will all be quite easy."

"As long as Miss Tuke is in charge," said Mr. Manders, "we will manage."

Miss Tuke arrived on Thursday evening with her van full of things for the gymkhana—bending poles, professionally painted red and white poles for the jumps, numbers for the competitors and stakes and rope to mark off the ring.

"Climb in," she said to Sue and Jinny. "We'll drive this lot down to the field."

"Actually," said Jinny, "we have more or less built the course."

"Good show," said Miss Tuke. "That's what I like, getting things done. Still, always room for improvement."

They improved for most of the evening, and by ten o'clock the jumps that Sue and Jinny had built were completely changed.

"Start the way they are for the Mini. One pole up for the Midi, and for the Maxi we'll add straw bales and change the centre jump into an in and out," Miss Tuke stated, hands on hips, when they had finished. "Showing classes first, round the outside of the jumps. Jumping next. Lunch break. Then games last of all. How are we for rosettes?"

"We made them," said Jinny, "out of plaited straw. Ken showed us how to plait it. I've drawn horses heads in different colours to stick in the middle of them so we'll know which is which."

"They're better than bought ones," said Sue.

"Great," said Miss Tuke. "And what about this cup?"

"Points for each class. Three for first, two for second and

one for third. Then all the points are added up and most points wins the cup," said Jinny.

"Make a scoreboard," warned Miss Tuke. "Stick it up where they can all see it, or we'll be here till next week squabbling about who's won. Justice must not only be done, it must be seen to be done."

"Will you present the cup?" Jinny asked.

"Lord, no! I'm the judge. Ask Mr. MacKenzie."

"Oh yes," agreed Sue. "He'd love to. He is coming. He was telling us about . . ."

Jinny kicked her hard on the ankle and quickly asked Miss Tuke when she thought her trek would reach Finmory.

"Should make it for eleven. Leave sharpish. Now, let's get these bending poles stacked away. Take them down to the yard. That should be nearest for you on Saturday morning."

Mr. MacKenzie, hearing them in his yard, came out in shirt sleeves and braces to see who it was.

"You'll be performing on Saturday?" he asked Miss Tuke.

"Judging," replied Miss Tuke sharply.

"Och, och," said Mr. MacKenzie, fixing Miss Tuke with his pale blue eyes. "It's surprised I am to hear you've the time for that, and the tinkers camping on your very doorstep."

"Scoundrels," snorted Miss Tuke. "If I set eyes on them I phone the police."

"Wise you are," said Mr. MacKenzie. "But what else would you be doing, a helpless wee waif like yourself."

"The girls would tell you the trouble we had with them."

"Not a word," lied Mr. MacKenzie.

"We did," exclaimed Jinny.

"Not a word did I hear of it," insisted Mr. MacKenzie. "So, come you in for a wee dram and be telling me yourself."

Jinny and Sue walked back to Finmory through an evening that was pastel shades of grey and mauve.

"Not tomorrow but the next day," said Sue.

"Rosettes to finish. Scoreboard for the points. I thought we could pin it on to the table where Mum's getting the food. Hammer to knock in the bending poles. Petra's trannie, which she won't know about because she's not here, for Musical Poles, and potatoes from the farm for the Potato Race."

"Biscuits to buy," added Sue, "and rolls."

"I'm worn out," said Jinny. "No wonder they need all those Brigadiers and Majors and troops to organise Wembley."

"And they have longer than a week to do it in," agreed Sue.

"But they don't have Miss Tuke," said Jinny.

By three o'clock on Friday afternoon they had done everything, except for buying biscuits and collecting the rolls which Mrs. Manders had ordered from Mrs. Simpson.

"We're riding in for them," Jinny said, when her mother reminded her about them.

"Don't leave it any later."

"Going now," said Jinny. "Sue's bringing in the horses."

They had almost reached Glenbost when Jinny was sure she could hear the sound of hooves.

"Listen," she said, interrupting Sue's account of a mounted paperchase during which she and Pippen had got totally lost. "Isn't that a horse?" Jinny stopped Shantih so that she could hear better.

They could both hear the sound of hooves coming towards them.

"Definitely," said Sue. "Who can it be?"

"Don't know," said Jinny, as Shantih goggled in the direction of the hoofbeats. "Can't be Miss Tuke. Anyway, it doesn't sound like ponies."

Bramble whinnied and a high-pitched neigh answered him. Then round the corner came two horses.

A heavy grey with a hogged mane and Roman nose was being ridden by a large girl who looked about eighteen or nineteen. Her blonde hair curled round a solid face. She was wearing an immaculately-cut riding jacket, breeches and boots. In one strong hand she held the grey's reins, with the other she gripped the reins of a black thoroughbred whose gleaming coat was slickered with white light as he danced and cavorted alongside the grey.

"Glory be!" the girl cried, in a rich, plum-pudding voice. "If it isn't Jinny. But how super to see you again. We were all in the Bahamas for the summer, and it was such a flying visit at New Year that I just didn't have a tiny minute to drop in. Of course, I didn't have the nags up with me so I knew you wouldn't really mind. But I must say, it is rather super to meet you like this."

Sue looked in surprise from the girl's smiling face to Jinny's scowling, clenched expression.

"Shantih has come on. Why, she looks quite presentable now. You have done her well. I'm utterly amazed."

Staring straight ahead, Jinny rode past the two horses and their rider.

"Well, er . . . good-bye," said Sue awkwardly, and trotted after Jinny.

The girl shouted something that Jinny couldn't quite make out. It sounded like, "See you," but she couldn't be sure.

"Not if I see you first," thought Jinny darkly.

"Who was that?" demanded Sue, catching up. "Why didn't you speak to her?"

"That was Clare Burnley and you could say that I hate her."

"She seemed to like you O.K."

"I can tell you now," said Jinny, "because I don't suppose it matters, not now. Last Easter, a pair of ospreys nested on the moors. You know how rare they are in Scotland. Well, I was supposed to be guarding their nest when Clare lured me away. While I was away with her, her rotten brother came and stole the eggs."

Sue gasped with satisfactory disgust.

"She knows I know and she'd the cheek to talk to me again."

"They're super horses," said Sue.

"The grey's called Huston and the black is her show horse called Jasper. She brings them both up from Sussex so she

38

can win the cups at Inverburgh Show. It was Clare Burnley that presuaded me to take Shantih to the show last year, long before she was anything like ready for a show. And she's got the nerve to say she'll see me!"

"She said," Sue repeated accurately, "see you tomorrow."

"Well she won't. It's the gymkhana."

"I think that's what she meant," said Sue.

CHAPTER FOUR

Jinny woke to the sound of pouring rain. She lay perfectly still, hearing it drumming against the window, storming over the rooftop and lashing through the trees. A wind moaned in from the sea, gusted over Finmory and howled over the moors.

"I don't believe it," Jinny thought. "There hasn't been a really wet day for weeks. It can't be. Not today."

She shut her eyes again and lay still.

"When I wake, the sun will be shining," she told herself. "When I open my eyes, it will be a blue day."

Jinny counted to ten, sat up, opened her eyes and the gale was still there. She jumped out of bed and stared down the garden.

Shantih, her coat stained rust-red with the downpour, was standing with her quarters turned against the wind. Her mane was soaked to strands of hair against her neck, her forelock plastered against her rain-carven face. Bramble's head was down, his lower lip touching the grass, his eyes screwed shut. He stood against the fury of wind and rain as his ancestors had stood against the ice age.

"Blooming, blasted weather!" said Jinny aloud, waking Sue. "Blasted rain!"

"What a day," said Sue. "What will you do? Phone Miss Tuke and cancel the whole thing?"

"No!" exclaimed Jinny. "We can't do that. It's to be a practice for the Inverburgh Show next Saturday. And there's the cup. Of course we can't cancel it. They don't cancel Badminton or the Grand National just because it's raining."

"Will Miss Tuke come?"

"If it was a weekday she would be trekking in it, so I don't see why she shouldn't. It's not all that heavy."

"Looks heavy enough to me," Sue said, and Mrs. Manders agreed with her.

"You're not going ahead with it?" she said in shocked tones when Jinny and Sue joined her in the kitchen.

"Of course," said Jinny. "We've all got wellies and oilskins. When you've organised a thing, you can't back down because of a little rain."

The phone rang and Jinny dashed to answer it.

"What's it doing with you?" demanded Miss Tuke's voice.

"Bit wet," admitted Jinny grudgingly.

"Pouring down with us. I've had Moira on the phone. She's still game. What do you think? I'll need to let them know if you want to call it off."

"Oh no! It's not nearly wet enough for that."

"Right you are," said Miss Tuke. "We'll be over. Trek forward."

"Was it Miss Tuke?" asked Mrs. Manders.

Jinny nodded. "Just checking that everything was O.K. here. They'll be over about eleven."

"Incredible," said Mrs. Manders.

"We'd better bring ours in before breakfast," said Jinny, wanting to escape from her mother. "Not that it will make any difference. Five minutes out in this and they'll be soaked again."

Sue and Jinny put on oilskins, sou'westers and wellingtons and launched themselves into the rain-swamped garden.

"Not so bad when you're out in it," said Jinny, running to the tackroom for halters.

Hearing them coming, Shantih and Bramble stampeded

to the gate where, nipping and kicking, they fought to get through first.

"Stand up with you," Jinny growled, struggling to get the halter over Shantih's ears as she reared her way through the gate. Running at her side, Jinny took her into the stable and shut her in her loosebox.

Glowering, ears pinned back, Bramble crashed his way into his stall.

"I'm drowned already," moaned Sue. "Gallons of rain pouring down my back."

"Banned," said Jinny. "Forbidden. For the rest of the day we must not mention the rain, on pain of excommunication."

Sue grinned. "O.K.," she said.

"No point in grooming just now," said Jinny. "Might as well go in and eat and then go down to the field."

Mrs. Manders fed them a breakfast of fried potato scone, bacon and egg.

"You'll need to dish out the lemonade from the car," suggested Jinny, hoping her mother was still willing.

"Thought hot soup from Thermoses as well."

"Yes. Even better."

"And I'll steward from the car," said Mike.

"You will not," said Jinny. "I've got plastic sheets to cover the scoreboards. You write underneath the plastic. But you'll need to bring the cup in the car. Put it behind the windscreen where people can see it. And they can collect their numbers from the car. You will all be there by eleven, won't you, so we can start whenever Miss Tuke arrives?"

"Sir! Yes, sir!" exclaimed Mike.

After breakfast, Jinny and Sue walked down to the field.

"At least the jumps are still standing," said Sue, as they went through the gate and began walking round the course. "By the time we reach the Maxi jumping, it will be really poached up."

"I know," agreed Jinny despondently. "Miss Tuke's Highlands could turn the Sahara into a quagmire, never mind this."

They brought the bending poles and the hammer from the farm, then, deciding there was nothing else they could do, they went back to Finmory to groom their horses.

"Useless," cried Jinny, after half an hour's dandying. "Sodden she is and sodden she will remain."

"They'll all be the same."

"Reckon so."

At a quarter to eleven, Jinny, holding a restless Shantih, and Sue on a sullen Bramble, were standing in Mr. MacKenzie's hay shed waiting for Miss Tuke and her trekkers, while the rain poured down as heavily as ever.

"Here they come," said Jinny, as Shantih, hearing the approaching ponies, began to paw at the floor of the shed.

"Be watching my good ground, now," warned Mr. MacKenzie, sack over his shoulders against the rain. "Keep that varmit under control."

Miss Tuke, in brilliant yellow oilskins, led the trek. Behind her came two bearded men in their early twenties riding dun Highlands.

"First two the trekkers," Jinny informed Sue. "The next two ladies are in the Trekking Club. Then Peter, Jim and George Hay. Peter's the oldest, on the black pony. He's quite good. Rode round the cross-country at Miss Tuke's. That's Moira Wilson on Snuff. He belongs to Moira. Very fast. And Sara Murdoch on Pym. He's her own Highland, but stubborn."

"Some day," Sara shouted, greeting Jinny. "What rain!"

"Rain?" said Jinny, staring about her. "I see no rain."

"We're drenched. Don't forget we've been riding for miles."

"I'll leave this fellow in one of your boxes," Miss Tuke said to Mr. MacKenzie. "Can't judge and ride. Jinny, lead on to the field. I'll be with you in a min."

Jinny swung herself up on to Shantih.

"This way," she shouted. "The gymkhana is down this way," and, making sure they were all following her, Jinny rode on.

Suddenly there was a rattling, crashing, engine noise behind them and lurching into the farmyard came a horsebox being driven by Clare Burnley.

"Oh, no!" cried Jinny. "Not her. She can't come. Not her."

"You can't send her home," said Sue. "She'll need to stay now she's here."

"Oh death," swore Jinny, and, turning her back on the horsebox, she led the trekkers into the field. The horsebox came lumbering after them.

There was a confused half-hour while the trekkers collected their numbers from the Manders' car, discovered the hot soup and decided to have it now instead of lunch time, and then had to nip round Mr. MacKenzie's yard trying to find suitable places to spend a penny.

"The first class," roared Miss Tuke, against the wind. "Best Turned Out Horse and Rider."

Clare Burnley led the grey, Huston, down the ramp of her box, tightened his girths, pulled down her stirrups and, mounting, rode into the ring.

Walking round the ring on Shantih, Jinny gazed despondently at the rest of the competitors—riding macs, anoraks and plastic raincoats were soaked, hard hats spouted waterfalls, tack was spongy, while Clare Burnley's white riding mac was just starting to darken, her tack glistened, and Huston gleamed as he stepped out with a sure stride.

"Beyond me," said Jinny, to no one in particular. "It is beyond me how she has the nerve to come here after last year. If I were judging, I would disqualify her."

Miss Tuke, after doing her best to inspect the tack and riders' turn-out, placed Clare Burnley first, Moira Wilson second and George Hay third.

Ken presented the plaited straw rosettes.

"Oh, how sweet," exclaimed Clare, taking hers. "I've never known a gymkhana where they couldn't afford to buy rosettes."

"No entry fees," snapped Miss Tuke. "All free."

"Forget that you won it," advised Ken. "Look on it as a thing of beauty, a light-bringer. That's what they used to be. To carry the light from one harvest to the next."

43

"Really?" said Clare. "But how sweet."

"Class two," announced Miss Tuke. "Horse and Rider Best Suited To Each Other. I've had a good look at you all, so trot on round until I make up my mind."

Shantih, fretting against the rain, struggled to canter. Grimly, Jinny held her back. Twice the bay Highland in front of them had lashed out, narrowly missing Shantih's leg.

"Steady, steady," muttered Jinny through clenched teeth, as Shantih fought to get her head down and buck.

"Walk," called Miss Tuke, and to Jinny's disgust she again gave the first prize to Clare. The second went to a nervous Trekking Club lady on a nursemaid Highland, and third to Sara Murdoch.

"Thought she might have given it to you, Shantih being the same colour as your hair," said Sue.

"No chance," said Jinny. "Miss Tuke thinks Shantih is THE most unsuitable horse of the year."

"Jumping classes next," organised Miss Tuke, and Jinny thought that the jumping was what really mattered—she had to show them all how Shantih had improved. She had to beat Clare Burnley.

"You may enter for either Mini, Midi or Maxi. Up to your honesty to choose the highest jumps you can manage. Sara, you are Maxi."

"Oh, but Miss Tuke I can't . . ."

"Maxi," decreed Miss Tuke. "Now Paul, you're first for the Mini."

One of the bearded trekkers trotted into the ring and bowed to Miss Tuke.

"Never before have I left the ground whilst balancing on a horse," he announced. "Feel privileged to be present."

As the non-jumpers did their best to make their ponies walk over the Mini jumps, Jinny sat on Shantih, staring crossly about her. Already Clare Burnley had six points. "And I've not got one," thought Jinny furiously.

A small figure was crouching against the wall. Jinny rode Shantih closer to it, and saw that it was the tinker boy who they had seen when they were catching Miss Tuke's ponies.

He was wearing the same ragged jacket and jeans. His black hair was sleeked down on to his head, and his face was shiny with rain. At his side was one of the brindled lurchers. It was sitting upright with the boy's arm round its shoulder. The boy's eyes were fixed on the pony in the ring, his expression one of rapt delight.

"Hi," said Jinny, riding up to him. "Isn't it wet?"

The boy flinched, his arm automatically swinging up to protect his head while the lurcher bared its teeth, snarling at Jinny.

"Not welcome," thought Jinny, and rode on.

Peter Hay was the first of the Maxi jumpers. He had two refusals and a bar down at the double. Moira on Snuff charged round the course and had four down. Mike and Ken rebuilt the jumps. Sara was next and had a refusal at every jump.

"Me next," said Sue. "Right now I'd give anything to be sitting on Pippen, warbled or not."

Bramble crabbed into the ring, his neck bent against the rain, and cat-jumped, tossing Sue on to his neck at every jump. At the fourth jump of bales and red poles, he slipped his shoulder and deposited Sue neatly into the mud, then stood gazing down at her with an innocent expression on his face.

"Mr. MacKenzie does not know what he's missing," moaned Sue, riding out of the ring after three refusals at the double.

"Don't worry," said Jinny. "He'll hear about it."

"Jinny Manders," shouted Miss Tuke, managing to boom and sound irritated at the same time. "We're waiting."

Jinny flurried into the ring at a sudden, ragged trot. In front of each of the jumps was a sea of poached mud. "Whatever will Mr. MacKenzie say," Jinny thought, feeling her reins slimy between her fingers, her hat biting into the back of her neck.

Miss Tuke blew her whistle and Shantih bounded forward of her own accord. Blinded by the rain, Jinny felt her soar skywards over the jump and, as soon as she touched down on the other side, she bucked. With a half-rear she

45

tore down the field to the next jump, cleared it effortlessly and raced on, totally out of control.

Round the foot of the field they went, and up the other side of the ring, Shantih taking the jumps like a steeple-chaser. At the top of the ring Jinny fought to turn her, but her reins were far too long and Shantih charged on out of the ring.

Tears of rage and frustration mixed with the rain streamed down Jinny's cheeks. She had been so sure that Shantih had stopped her uncontrollable galloping, that she had learnt how to jump calmly and sensibly. And now, to behave like that in front of Miss Tuke, the pony trekkers, and worst of all, Clare Burnley . . . Jinny groaned with despair as she at last managed to bring Shantih to a trot and then to a walk.

"Idiot horse," Jinny told her. "They are all right. You are mad."

Shantih turned her head, drifting sideways against the rain. Her ears were flattened to her head and her eyes gogg-ling with nervous excitement.

"Disaster," said Sue, riding up on Bramble.

"But you saw her. You saw how she had improved—and now back to her stupid nonsense," and, staring through the sheeting rain, Jinny watched Clare Burnley jump a clear round, her showjumper treating the Maxi course with con-tempt.

"She's won," said Sue. "No doubt about it, she's the best."

"She shouldn't be here," exclaimed Jinny. "Nine points! Shes got nine points for the cup. No one else has had a chance."

When the rosettes for the jumping had been presented, Miss Tuke announced an hour for lunch and added that the soup flasks had been replenished.

The trekkers crowded round the car, grateful for the hot soup, and suddenly Jinny remembered the tinker boy. She looked round for him and saw that he was still crouching against the wall, with his arm round the dog. She gave Shantih to Sue, and filling a cup with soup and taking a cheese roll, walked across to him.

"Here," she said, keeping a wary eye on the lurcher. "I've brought you some soup."

"Don't want it," said the boy. "I've not got no money."

"It's free," said Jinny. "My father paid for all the food. Go on, take it."

Without looking up at Jinny, the boy stretched up his hand and took the cup and the roll from Jinny. He drained the hot soup in one gulp, tore the roll into two pieces, cramming one half into his own mouth and giving the other bit to his dog.

"Do you like ponies?" Jinny asked him.

The boy nodded, wiping his mouth on his jacket sleeve.

"Can you ride?" Jinny asked, when he didn't speak.

"Aye. We have the ponies sometimes and we ride them."

"And dogs?" said Jinny.

"Zed's mine," said the boy, clutching the snarling dog closer to his side. "He works best for me."

Suddenly Miss Tuke's heavy hand descended on Jinny's shoulder.

"Get out of here," she shouted at the boy. "Get back to your camp and stay there."

Cringing, the boy scrambled to his feet. The lurcher leapt at Miss Tuke, snarling, lips rolled back, but the boy kept a tight hold on its collar.

"He's not doing any harm," exclaimed Jinny indignantly. "He's 'spectators welcome'. The only one who has come. He can stay if he wants to."

"Leave him here and the next thing he'll be crawling about the farm, picking up what he can find. Now be off with you."

"No," said Jinny. "He's got as much right to be here as anyone else." But already the tinker boy had swarmed over the wall and was running across the fields, down to the sea.

"What a beastly thing to do," stated Jinny, scowling at Miss Tuke. "What a foul, rotten thing to do."

"Nonsense. Go back to Finmory and find your tack gone. You'll sing a different song then, my girl."

"He was only enjoying himself. Sitting watching the ponies."

"Are you running this gymkhana or are you not? If you are, it's about time you came and gave us a hand in the ring."

Silently, Jimmy supposed that Miss Tuke might be right. She followed her across the field to help her father and Mike to knock in the poles for Musical Poles.

"At least they all seem to be enjoying themselves," said Mr. Manders, taking the hammer from Jinny and knocking the poles in himself. "Clare Burnley has star quality."

Ponies and riders were grouped around the lowered ramp of Clare's box. She stood inside the box, regaling her audience with tales from her horsy past. Jinny could hear her loud, arrogant voice and the trekkers' admiring chatter.

"She's telling them about all the cups she's won," said Jinny grimly. "And when she gets back to England she'll tell them about how she won this cup, bringing her posh horse to a gymkhana like this."

"It is a bit your own fault," said her father. "Didn't you think of putting some sort of limit on who could enter?"

"Only allowed to enter if you're totally hopeless," suggested Mike.

"Shut up," warned Jinny. "I am not in the mood to be teased. I am totally and utterly low."

Clare wasn't placed in Musical Poles. The lady from the Trekking Club, who had been second in the Suitable Horse class, won it. Her pony trotted round, obviously listening to Petra's transistor with both ears. The second Mr. Manders switched the music off, the pony bolted for a pole and stood stock still beside it. All its rider had to do was to put her hat on the pole. Moira was second and Peter third. Jinny was first out, since Shantih refused to go near the circle of poles.

But Clare won the bending and the potato race.

"Of course, he's not what one would choose for games but, let's face it, there's not much competition here today," said Clare, to one of the bearded trekkers.

"I really think you're wonderful the way you ride. Make it look so easy. Still, I expect you've been at it since you were a kid."

"You might say I was more or less born in the saddle," confided Clare.

"Puke, double puke," thought Jinny, overhearing the conversation.

Mr. MacKenzie, sourly surveying his churned-up field, presented the cup to Clare.

"Thanks frightfully," said Clare.

To Jinny's disgust, she held it above her head with both hands while everyone clapped.

For a second, Jinny saw herself taking it from Mr. MacKenzie. A real cup. The first her family had ever won. The first Shantih had ever won.

"It should have been mine. I should have won it. Not her. Not that Clare Burnley," thought Jinny sullenly, not clapping.

"You didn't even win one point," said the voice in Jinny's head. "Shantih was just as wild as ever."

"It was the weather," protested Jinny. "She was upset by the rain. It was that Clare Burnley."

"You wouldn't have won it anyway."

"If she hadn't come, everything would have been different."

Clare Burnley rode out of the ring and came straight up to Jinny.

"I really have enjoyed myself," she said. "When one is used to big shows one really does so enjoy a little do like this. Utterly fascinating. Thank you so much for organising it." Clare held out her hand to Jinny.

"I can't," thought Jinny. "I cannot shake her hand. I cannot."

"Oh," said Clare. "Having a tiny sulk, are we?"

"It wasn't fair," said Jinny, the words bursting out of her. "It wasn't fair, bringing a horse like Huston here. It's not fair taking them to Inverburgh Show, but to bring him here and carry off the cup . . ."

"Dearie me," laughed Clare. "That's what's wrong, is it? The cup? Goodness, I'd give the wretched thing to you. Means absolutely nothing to me. I've got dozens of the things."

"Clare," called the bearded trekker, whom Jinny had heard talking to Clare earlier in the day. "We're going back now. Do give me your phone number and we'll see if we can fix something up."

"In the book," Clare replied, turning to ride over to him.

As she rode away, she looked back over her shoulder at Jinny. He face, half-turned, seemed to Jinny to lose its smooth mask of monied security, was suddenly naked, her eyes coldly calculating, her mouth tight and grasping.

"But, of course, if you want to win a cup for yourself there's always Inverburgh Show."

CHAPTER FIVE

Sunday, after Saturday's rain, was a grey day, as if the gale had washed the colour out of the world. As Sue and Jinny wandered down to the field to clear up the remains of the gymkhana, the moors stretched in greyness to the mist-shrouded mountains. The fields reaching down to the sea were grey-green, even the jet shards of the cliffs were toned to dark grey shades, standing out from a sea of liquid-grey metal.

"Miss Tuke's coming for them tonight," Jinny said, pulling the bending poles out of the ground. "We'd better take them down to the farm and stack them in the hay shed."

"Couldn't we just leave them here?" asked Sue.

"Leave them another night and hordes of tinkers will descend from the hills to steal them."

"Right enough," said Sue.

"I don't mean it," said Jinny. "I don't mean it at all. Tinkers aren't crawling about waiting to pounce on things. That's all in Miss Tuke's head."

"You don't believe they ever steal things, do you?" said

Sue, as they carried the bending poles, the red and white posts and the rope and stakes down to Mr. MacKenzie's. "You just imagine them raggle-taggle-gypsy-oing. They're not really like that. They do steal. That's why people don't like them, don't want them camping near them."

"Not steal," insisted Jinny, as they went back and forward between the field and the yard. "Maybe poach or lift an old bucket that's lying about a back door, but that's not stealing. I think Miss Tuke bringing her ponies down from the hill because there are tinkers camping at the next farm, is plain silly. Fancy thinking they would steal them for meat!"

"Do you know, in England some native pony breeders have nearly stopped breeding ponies because the meat men will pay more for a pure-bred pony than the people who are wanting to show them. It's not a few pounds, it's hundreds."

Jinny felt her stomach clench tight with a sudden spasm of fear. The fact of horses being sold for slaughter was so terrible that Jinny couldn't even allow herself to think about it.

"I don't believe you," she told Sue.

"Choose how," said Sue. "It's the truth. No one near us would dream of sending their pony to a sale, just in case."

Jinny clanked down the milk can she was carrying at the byre door, and from the door of the farmhouse Mr. MacKenzie appeared in his Sabbath suit.

"I'll be filling it for you after church," he said.

"We'll fetch it this afternoon," said Jinny. "Miss Tuke is coming over tonight to collect her poles. O.K. if we leave them there?"

"I'll have the eye open for her," said Mr. MacKenzie. "It was the disaster of a day you had yesterday."

"A wash out," said Sue.

"Now it wasn't exactly the rain I was thinking of, although you'd plenty of that right enough. It was more the little matter of the cup."

Jinny scowled across at him. She had known he would have something to say about it.

51

"The likes of yourselves setting up the wee gymkhana so that her ladyship can add another cup to her collection!"

"How was I to know she'd be here?" asked Jinny indignantly.

"Och now, the halfwit would have known that a cup would have drawn Clare Burnley to it. Like a moth to a candle that one is for the cups."

"I never even thought of her being back at Craigvaar," Jinny said, as Ewan MacKenzie, one of Mr. MacKenzie's sons, drove into the yard to take his parents to church.

When Jinny and Sue had finished stacking the poles in the hay shed, they gathered up the litter that had been left behind in the field and did their best to stamp down the ploughed earth around the jumps.

"He won't be very keen to let you hold another gymkhana," said Sue, surveying their efforts.

"Indeed no," said Jinny, being Mr. MacKenzie. "I just hope he'll let me go on jumping here this week. We've got to practise for Inverburgh. I've got to practise every day."

"Not today," Sue said. "You never jump your horse the day after a gymkhana."

"We'll go for a ride then," said Jinny. "Though I don't think it would make any difference to Shantih. Maybe she was too fresh yesterday."

"Maybe," said Sue.

Privately, Sue thought that Shantih would always be too impetuous to make a showjumper. She didn't think that anything Jinny did would make her completely reliable, but she knew Jinny too well to mention it.

As they walked up the drive to Finmory, a sports car scorched past them and stopped at the front door. A young woman in a patchwork tweed coat got out.

"It's Nell Storr. She buys our pottery," said Jinny, waving.

"So it is," said Sue, remembering Nell from last summer.

"I'm not coming in," stated Nell. "We're late as it is. Root out Ken. Tell him I'm here."

The front door opened and Ken, with Kelly at his heels, walked out.

"Bundle in," said Nell.

"Where are you going?" Jinny demanded, instantly alert to think that Ken was going somewhere that she didn't know about.

"Over to Melden," said Nell, as Kelly jumped into the back of the car and Ken folded himself into the seat beside her. "Fabulous woman there. Paints pebbles. Out of this world."

"Take peace," said Ken. "I'll be back tomorrow or Tuesday. Yesterday was too much. The screams of those wretched horses."

"What does he mean, screaming horses?" asked Sue, as they drove away.

"At the gymkhana," explained Jinny. "Ken thinks that horses with bits in their mouths are screaming all the time, only our ears can't hear them."

"Oh," said Sue politely.

After lunch they caught Shantih and Bramble and rode to Glenbost.

"Will the moors be much too wet?" Sue asked hopefully.

"Much," said Jimmy, "but we can go on along the road for a bit further."

"O.K.," said Sue, and they trotted on, following the road to Ardtallon.

Since it was Sunday, the road was quieter than usual and they were able to ride side by side, discussing ways in which Shantih could be turned into a steady showjumper before Saturday.

"She can jump higher than Clare's horse, honestly she can," Jinny was saying, when they heard the roar of a heavy vehicle coming up behind them.

Sue pulled Bramble back, tucking him in behind Shantih, and Jinny glanced round to see a crashing, rattling mass of cattle float bearing down on them.

"Going far too fast," Jinny thought. "Don't know who it belongs to. No one round here."

The float careered past, being driven by a man in a tweed jacket and cap to match. As he passed Jinny he turned his head to stare at Shantih.

"He'll know us again," Jinny thought, steadying Shantih who had leapt forward, breaking into a sudden canter.

"Road pig," said Sue.

Suddenly a dog leapt over the dry stone wall that separated the moorland from the road.

"Look out!" Jinny screamed uselessly.

The float driver made no attempt to stop or swerve. His front wheel caught the dog and flung it into the air where, to Jinny's horrified gaze, it seemed to hang, a spread-eagled, stuffed toy, before it thwacked down into the road.

They galloped to where it lay, jumped down and crouched beside it. It was a large brindled lurcher – one of the tinker's dogs.

"Not dead," said Jinny, feeling its heart. "Unconscious. Been hit on its back leg."

There was a bleeding gash on the dog's upper thigh. It lay strangely twisted, making Jinny think that it might have damaged its spine.

"And he didn't even stop!" cried Sue.

A noise above them made them look up, as the tinker boy hurtled over the wall to land beside them.

"Zed!" he cried, kneeling down beside the dog, clutching its head into his knees. "What did it?"

"Cattle float," said Jinny. "We saw it. Your dog jumped over the wall in front of it."

"Me da will shoot him," said the boy.

"Don't talk so soft," said Jinny sharply. "Come on, we've got to get him to the vet. If it had to happen, it couldn't have happened in a better place. The vet's house is just round the next corner. Better try and do something with his leg before we try to move him. Come on, help me."

They made a thick pad out of paper handkerchiefs and Jinny pressed it against the gash in the dog's leg, while Sue took off the tee shirt she was wearing under her sweater and they wrapped it round the paper pad. But it was no sooner in place than the blood had soaked through it and was trickling down the dog's leg again.

Jinny took off her anorak, laid it on the ground, and they

lifted the dog on to it. As they moved the dog it gave a half snarl, half yelp, then lay back unconscious again.

"If you each take a side," Jinny said to Sue and the tinker boy, "you can carry him between you, and I'll ride on to the vet's and let him know we're coming."

Jinny cantered along the road, and trotted up the path, with its border of garden gnomes, to the vet's house. A man's face appeared at the window and, with a surge of relief, Jinny recognised Jim Rae, the vet. He was at the door as Jinny dismounted.

"A dog's been hit by a cattle float," Jinny gasped. "The others are bringing him in."

"Round to the surgery," said the vet, lifting a ring of keys from a hook by the door and leading the way to a surgery built on to the side of his house. "There's a loosebox round the back, put your horse in there."

Jinny led Shantih round to an old-fashioned loosebox and left her.

"I'll take your end," she said to Sue, meeting them on the path and taking the side of the anorak that Sue had been holding. "You can put Bramble in with Shantih."

Jinny and the tinker boy carried the dog into the surgery.

"Let's have him on the table," said the vet. "That's the way. Easy now." Carefully, they slid the dog off the anorak on to the table.

"Now, let's see," said the vet, beginning to examine the lurcher.

Sue joined them and they stood silently watching, staring at the vet's face for any sign of how seriously the dog had been hurt.

"Well, you're lucky," said Jim Rae at last. "Nasty tear in his leg, but apart from that, nothing broken. I'll get him stitched up before he comes round."

With sure movements the vet stitched up the dog's leg. Watching, Jinny didn't feel squeamish the way she did when she watched operations on film. It was too interesting—so interesting that she forgot about everything except the vet's skill and the need to help the injured animal.

"There," said the vet. "How's that?"

"Perfect," said Jinny.

"A-plus," said Sue.

But the tinker boy never spoke. His dark eyes were fixed unblinkingly on his dog.

"I take it the dog belongs to our friend here," said the vet. "So not much point in telling you to make sure he's kept quiet for the next day or two. He'll be off after the rabbits again as soon as he can run. Isn't that so?"

"Aye," muttered the boy. "Jake'll make him."

Suddenly the dog shuddered and scrambled to its feet. With a cry of joy the boy dashed forward and flung his arms round the dog's neck, burying his face against the dog's shoulder, whimpering against the dog with small cries of delight.

"He'll do fine," said the vet, lifting the dog down. "Keep him away from lorries in future."

The boy gave one quicksilver glance round the faces that were watching him, ducked his head to the side with a quick jerk and, holding his dog by the collar, bolted out before anyone realised what he was going to do.

"Well," said Sue in disgust. "He didn't even say thank you."

"If you'd been brought up by Jake Brodie you wouldn't be saying thank you, you'd be getting out while the going was good," said the vet, beginning to clear up.

"Do you know the tinkers?" asked Jinny.

"I've seen to their animals from time to time," said the vet. "Jake's a hard man. I wouldn't cross him if I could help it." And Jinny remembered how the boy had flung up his arm to protect his face when she had spoken to him yesterday.

"Will the dog be all right?" asked Sue.

"Good chance," said the vet. "They're as tough as the kids, the ones who survive."

"What about the stitches?" asked Sue. "Won't you need to take them out?"

The vet shook his head. "Knew there was no chance of the tinks bringing him back. The stuff I've stitched him up with will dissolve once the wound has healed."

"I'll bring the money tomorrow," said Jinny.

"Forget it," said the vet. "I daresay there'll be a couple of hares left on my doorstep before they move on."

"Yuch," said Jinny.

"Very tasty," said the vet.

That evening, Jinny, Sue and Mike went down to the farm to wait for Miss Tuke and to help her load the poles into her van.

"Half-past nine," said Mike, when they had been waiting for ages. "Did she say when she'd be here?"

"Not exactly. She only said when they'd finished trekking."

"Must be having an evening trek," said Mike.

It was almost ten before Miss Tuke drove into the yard and jerked to a stop. She jumped out of the van and came striding across the yard. They could see at once there was something wrong. Her eyes were blazing, every hair on her head seemed electric with fury and her lips worked as she ranted to herself.

"Been hanging around for me, have you?" she asked. "Sorry about that. Had one awful day. It has happened. Knew it would. Two of my ponies gone."

"Gone?" echoed Jinny. "You mean broken out?"

"I mean," said Miss Tuke, "what I say. Gone."

Mr. MacKenzie, having heard the van, had come out to join them.

"Yesterday. Last night. Don't know. They weren't there this morning when I went to feed them."

"It'll be those broken-down old hedges," suggested Mr. MacKenzie. "It's time you were after taking a darning needle to them."

"Nothing could get out of the hill paddock," stated Miss Tuke. "Wire right round and neither Polly nor Moll could jump four feet to save themselves. Of course, the first thing I thought of was that they'd got out somehow. Organised the trekkers to help and not a break in the hedge. Gate was shut."

"You'd be searching the moor for them? They're cunning

blighters, the Highlands. Could have crept through somewhere."

"Searched for miles. That's where I've been. Not a sign. Phoned the police. P.C. Hutchins has all the details in his notebook and, if it's left to him, there they'll stay until he's eaten the poor brutes in his breakfast sausages."

"You mean you think they've been stolen?" gasped Jinny. "But who would steal your ponies? Who?"

"Well you may ask. The very ones you were feeding up with soup yesterday. That's what I'd say."

"That boy wouldn't steal anything," exclaimed Jinny. "He wouldn't steal ponies."

"You think it is the tinks?" asked Mr. MacKenzie.

"No doubt," said Miss Tuke. "I've been round to Alec McGowan's. He took me over to the camp and, of course, there wasn't a sign of a horse anywhere near them. That rogue, Jake, sneering at me. I'll be back tomorrow and P.C. Hutchins will be with me."

"What else will you do? Where else will you look?" asked Jinny.

Miss Tuke flung her hands wide, shaking her head with rage and frustration.

"They could be anywhere. Never see another trace." And Miss Tuke began to load the poles into her van, crashing them in as if they were the horse thieves.

"It's absolutely terrible," said Jinny, as they walked back to Finmory. "I can't believe it, honestly I can't."

"The police will do something about it," said Mike. "They don't let anyone go about pinching other people's things."

"I'm going down to see Shantih," Jinny said when they reached Finmory, making it obvious that she wanted to go alone. Leaving the others, she sped across the garden to the horses' field.

"Shantih," she called. "Shantih."

A low whinny answered her as Shantih lifted her head from grazing and, with pricked ears and dark eyes, bright at the sound of Jinny's voice, came stepping through the grass to wait for Jinny at the gate.

At the sound of Shantih's whinny, relief flooded warm and sweet through the whole of Jinny's being. Ever since she had heard that Miss Tuke's ponies had been stolen she had been frozen with fear that Shantih would not be in her field when they got back to Finmory.

Again Shantih whinnied, calling to Jinny.

"If there were a million horses and I heard Shantih, I'd know it was her," Jinny thought, as she climbed over the gate and flung her arms round Shantih's neck.

"Shantih," she whispered against her horse's neck, and suddenly tears were running down Jinny's face. She had been so afraid that the field would be empty, that she would never see Shantih again.

"I thought they'd stolen you too," she told Shantih, as she rubbed her eyes dry against the back of her hand. "I couldn't bear it if anything happened to you."

Jinny wished desperately that Ken and Kelly hadn't gone away with Nell Storr. "Kelly would hear if anyone came near Finmory," Jinny thought, and she shuddered at the thought of the tinker they'd called Jake creeping around Finmory House at night. Jinny imagined the horse thieves as silent shapes in the darkness, coming down to the horses' field to lead Shantih and Bramble away and sell them for meat.

Someone moved on the other side of the gate. Jinny leapt back, screaming.

"Jinny," said her father's voice crossly. "I thought this was what you'd be doing, standing down here imagining all sorts of nonsense. Come on in. It's nearly eleven."

"Whee!" said Jinny, her heart thumping in her throat. "I thought you were the horse thieves."

Hurriedly she took a piece of carrot from her pocket and gave it to Shantih. Bramble came bustling across to get his share.

"Move it," said Mr. Manders.

Jinny walked back to Finmory, her arm linked through her father's arm.

"I never thought of it before," she said. "As long as they were in their field I was sure they were safe."

59

"Perhaps Miss Tuke is wrong," suggested Mr. Manders. "Maybe they have only strayed."

"Don't think so," said Jinny, shaking her head. "She was sure the ponies had been stolen. It's not like Miss Tuke to panic over nothing."

CHAPTER SIX

"Dry day," thought Jinny, as she opened her eyes to a bright morning. She thought, "Inverburgh Show. The cup. Clare Burnley. School Shantih over low jumps. Steady her," all in quick succession, all muddled together.

She stretched, sat up in bed, glancing across at Sue who was still asleep, then Jinny jumped out of bed and leant out of her open bedroom window.

"Shantih!" she called. "Shantih!"

For the first second, Jinny didn't believe her own eyes, for of course Bramble and Shantih must be in their field. Of course they must. They always were, always.

"Shantih," Jinny called again, her voice high-pitched with fear.

Deluging back into Jinny's memory came the recollection of the horse thieves who had stolen two of Miss Tuke's ponies.

"Shantih!" Jinny screamed.

The field gate was shut. They hadn't pushed it open and escaped that way. From her window there was only one corner of the field that Jinny couldn't see. It was possible that they might be there, but Jinny knew with a clemmed certainty that Shantih would never stay tucked into the corner, out of sight, when she was calling her. Bramble might, if he was on strike, but not Shantih. Not Shantih.

Jinny tore off her nightdress, pulled on sweater and jeans, forced her feet into sandshoes still laced from the night before, and hurtled through the house to the back door. Her hands struggled to turn the key, then she was running as she had never run before, down the garden, past the stables to the horses' field.

Jinny vaulted the gate, went on blindly until she was standing in the middle of the empty field.

"They've broken out," she told herself, and ran round the hedges looking for a place where they could have pushed their way through. But there was no gap with broken branches and tell-tale hoof prints. The hedge was as strong as it had always been.

"Shantih," screamed Jinny, "Shantih!" as if her voice could conjure her horses from the empty air. "Bramble!"

Jinny turned back, her legs suddenly too weak to carry her, her arms hanging uselessly by her sides. She reached the gate and leant against it. Out of her mouth came a sobbing groan of shock and misery.

"What's wrong?" demanded Sue's voice. "What on earth's the matter with you? Why are you going on like that?"

The sound of Sue's sharp efficient tones cut through Jinny's hysteria. She pushed her hair back from her face, gulped hard, trying to speak.

"They've gone. I knew last night. I should have brought them in. Stayed up to guard them. The meat men have got them."

"They'll only have broken out," Sue said, staring round the empty field. "Pippen does all the time. Once he was nearly on the motorway. We'll get them back."

"The gate was shut and there's nowhere in the hedge where they could have got out."

"They could have jumped out," insisted Sue.

"They never have before," said Jinny. "Why should they now? Why last night, just when Miss Tuke has had her ponies stolen?"

"Let's look down on the shore," said Sue, and began to run down the path to the sea.

Jinny followed her, not because she had any hope of finding Shantih, but because for the moment she couldn't think what else she could do, except to follow Sue and for a few more minutes cling to the hope that Shantih and Bramble might be there, might only have strayed. But Jinny was sure she hadn't strayed. Already she was sure that Shantih and Bramble had been stolen.

The shore was bright with sunlight shimmering on sea and sand. The gulls' cries ripped the early morning silence. The black cliffs were withdrawn and menacing against the glittering water.

There was no trace of Arab or Highland; no crescent hoofprints marked the sand, no chestnut shape picked fastidiously at the seaweed, no black bulk, lips drawn back, fed on the sea holly.

Jinny stood perfectly still, staring out over the deserted shore to the impersonal expanse of the sea. The horror of the first shock began to die down, to settle into a leaden weight in her chest.

"Shall we search round the cliffs?" suggested Sue.

"No point," said Jinny. "If they were here we'd see the hoofprints. We'd better get back. Phone Miss Tuke. Tell Dad. Phone the police."

Jinny ran steadily back to Finmory. She found her father standing in the pottery, still gritty with early morning, a mug of coffee in his hand.

"Shantih and Bramble have gone," Jinny said. "They didn't break out. The gate was shut. Someone's been here in the night and taken them away."

Mr. Manders looked in astonished surprise at Jinny's pale face, her eyes stretched wide and her mouth tight, holding back tears.

"The same men that stole Miss Tuke's," said Jinny. "Must be."

"Why would they want to do that, to come here?" asked her father. "It's much more likely that they've got out somehow. Probably gone down to Mr. MacKenzie's. They'll be down there now, eating his hay. That's much more probable."

"I'll phone him first," said Jinny, "just in case. Then I'll phone Miss Tuke."

Mr. MacKenzie hadn't seen Shantih or Bramble. They were not in his yard.

"Now don't you be letting that imagination of yours go galloping off with you," he said to Jinny. "It's on the moor they'll be. Gone for a wee visit to my Shetlands. It's the day for the visiting."

"There's no way they could have got out unless they'd jumped out, and if they'd been as excited as that I'd have heard them galloping about."

"Now wait you a minute," said Mr. MacKenzie, his voice suddenly serious. "It's now it's coming back into my head. I'd to be shouting at the dogs last night. Woke me with their barking, so they did."

"Didn't you go down to see what was wrong?"

"I'd the wee look out of my window and not a thing stirring, so I was thinking it would be a fox they'd heard, but now I'm thinking you should be giving the police a wee ring. It's not like Betsy to be barking for nothing."

"Then why didn't you go down and find out what she was barking at?" demanded Jinny, and slammed the phone down.

Jinny phoned Miss Tuke next.

"Blasted tinkers," she said. "It's them. I'm sure of it. Phone the police or get your father to do it. Pay more attention to him. I'm meeting P.C. Hutchins at ten and we're going over to the tinkers' camp. They'll deny everything, of course, but we may pick up some clues."

"Shall we come with you?" asked Jinny.

"No point. I'll let you know what happens. You get on the move. Scout about. Try Glenbost. Someone may have heard something strange last night."

"We will," said Jinny.

"Blasted, thieving tinks," said Miss Tuke again, before she rang off.

Mr. Manders phoned the police station at Ardtallon to report what had happened.

"They want details of the missing horses," he said, giving the phone to Jinny.

"You'll be knowing Miss Tuke at the trekking?" the

63

policeman asked, after he had taken down the descriptions.

"She's had ponies stolen too," said Jinny.

"We're making a visit to the tinkers' camp this morning," said the policeman. "I'll have the look about for your two while we're there."

"It might not be the tinkers," said Jinny. "It might be properly organised horse thieves."

"Indeed it might," said the policeman. "Or then again it might be yourselves are needing to take a wee walk round your hedges."

"Miss Tuke has wire round hers."

"So she was telling me, but I'm thinking you should both be taking a walk over the moors, just in case they're wandering about up there."

Jinny sat at the breakfast table crumbling the piece of toast which she knew she wasn't going to eat.

"They all believe they've strayed," she thought. "But I know they've been stolen. I know it."

It was almost as if the air round the field gate had still held some echo of the night's happenings; some turbulence left by the strangers coming in the dark, leading away the startled, unwilling horses; some message left behind that Jinny had been able to understand.

"I'll take you down to the village after breakfast," Mr. Manders said. "We'll ask around and see if anyone heard anything last night."

"And we'll talk to Mr. MacKenzie," said Jinny. "He might remember more about his dogs barking."

But when they drove past the farm there was no sign of Mr. MacKenzie.

"Stop on the way back," said Mr. Manders, driving on.

In the village they went first to Mrs. Simpson's shop. Drinking in the details to be retold to all her customers, Mrs. Simpson shook her head regretfully.

"Never a murmur did I hear," she said, and called her husband from the back shop. But he too had heard nothing unusual.

"Miss Tuke as well," moaned Mrs. Simpson, enjoying

herself. "That ordinary, decent people can't sleep in their beds without such things going on is a shame on us all!"

Sue and Jinny went to ask at the schoolhouse while Mr. Manders spoke to the men at the garage.

"Nothing," said Jinny, knowing from her father's face that the garage men hadn't been able to tell him anything either.

"We'll try some of the crofts," said Mr. Manders. "No harm in asking. If Mr. MacKenzie's dogs were disturbed there's a chance that someone else heard whatever disturbed them. But be polite," he warned.

It took ages asking at each croft. The crofters all knew Jinny and Shantih and had to be told every detail, but no one could help them.

"Poor Mrs. Simpson," said Mr. Manders, when they had been round all the crofts. "She won't be able to tell them her hot news. They'll all have heard it."

They drove back to Finmory in silence.

"If only Mr. Mackenzie had got up to find out what his dogs were barking at," said Sue, as they got out of the car in the farmyard.

"Don't start," warned Jinny. "Don't start 'if onlying'. Does no good. Too late for that."

"It's not a thing more I can be telling you," said Mr. MacKenzie. "When I heard them barking I took a look out of the window and not a thing was stirring, so I gave them a bit of a shout and back I went to bed."

"What shall we do next?" demanded Jinny. "Where shall we look next? Now, this minute, someone has Shantih. I've got to find her NOW, before . . ." but Jinny couldn't go on.

"Maybe Miss Tuke and the police force will have found them with the tinkers. She'll be more than a match for the tinkers, that one. It's Jake himself will be turning pale when he sees her coming."

"But what can we do?" repeated Jinny.

"Have you had the look over the hill?" suggested Mr. MacKenzie. "You be finding my Shetlands and I'm thinking you'll be finding that mare of yours."

"Take us ages on foot," said Jinny, but it was a last flickering hope; a useless activity to fill in the eternity of the afternoon.

"If your father would be driving you over to Ewan's, you could be taking his ponies. They're a couple of idle beggars. A jaunt over the hill would be doing them no damage."

Jinny remembered the two heavy, dun Highlands that Mr. MacKenzie and his son Ewan rode when they rounded up Mr. MacKenzie's herd of Shetlands and brought them down from the hill for the market each year.

"Could you take us over?"

"If we go now," her father said.

"Right," said Jinny.

Ewan MacKenzie's farm was about six miles away. When they drove into the yard, Ewan was waiting for them.

"Scoot out," said Mr. Manders. "I'll be here for hours if they lure me into the kitchen, and I must get some work done."

Sue and Jinny scooted out and Mr. Manders drove away.

"He's very busy," Jinny explained.

"That's the pity," said Ewan. "Maggie's got the teapot on. We'd the phone call from the old man telling us your troubles, so I've brought the two of them in for you, and it's welcome you are to have the use of them. Be keeping them at the farm while you're needing them."

"Thanks very much," said Jinny. "Mr. MacKenzie thinks that they might be on the hill with his Shetlands, so we're going to ride up and look."

"It's the terrible business altogether. Come you both in and be telling us about it."

Reluctantly, Jinny and Sue followed Ewan into the dark farm kitchen. His wife was pouring out cups of strong black tea and setting them on the table with plates of scones and cake.

It was nearly two before they escaped and went with Ewan to the hay shed, where two carthorsy Highland ponies were standing, tied to the shed posts, munching hay. They were both duns, with dense manes twisted into witch knots and tails woven with dead bracken and thorn twigs.

Ewan brought saddles and bridles. The leather was bone dry and the metal rusty. He swung the saddles on to the ponies' backs, sending up clouds of dust, and then crammed the bar snaffles into their mouths.

"Aye," he said, "they're canny beasts. No just what you're used to, but they'll carry you safe over the bogs, so they will."

He gave the reins of one of the Highlands to Jinny. "That's Jock," he said. "And this is Belle." He handed Belle's reins to Sue.

Ewan waited until Sue and Jinny had mounted.

"Aye, it's fine you'll be on those two," he said. "And be letting me know when you find your own."

"Will do," promised Jinny. "Thanks very much. Cheerio."

Belle and Jock lifted one slow, sober hoof after the other as they made their way up the hillside.

"Not fast," said Sue, her heels raising a dust storm from Belle's sides.

"But sure," said Jinny, as she allowed Jock to pick his own way over the rough ground. She knew it didn't matter. If they were on racehorses it wouldn't make any difference. Shantih and Bramble weren't on the moor. Jinny was only there because she didn't know what else to do. Didn't know where else to look for Shantih. Ken would be home in the evening. He might know.

Eventually they found the Shetlands, clustered together in a sheltered hollow. Some of the mares were stretched out on the grass, enjoying the spring sunshine, while others were grazing. One whinnied a warning as Sue and Jinny rode up.

There was no sign of Shantih or Bramble. It was obvious that they hadn't been near the Shetlands.

"Not here," said Sue.

"If Shantih had been loose up here she'd have found the Shetlands," said Jinny. "May as well get back home."

They rode back to Finmory, Jock and Belle moving at their own deliberate pace. Jinny knew from the gathering dusk that it must be quite late. Soon it would be a day and a night since Shantih and Bramble had been stolen.

Jinny gazed into the future. By the summer would she look back on yesterday as the last day she had seen Shantih? The last time she had seen Bramble—dear, comfortable, solid Bramble? This Easter be remembered all her life as the Easter when Shantih was stolen and never recovered? Jinny howled wolf-terror over the darkening moors, for it could be that way. It was only too possible that she would never see Shantih or Bramble again.

"Do you mind?" said Sue. "Going on like a raving idiot. That isn't going to help. We had to search the moors in case they were there with the Shetlands. Now we know for sure they aren't on the moors we can start and search for them in other places."

"Like what other places?" said Jinny miserably.

Sue didn't reply.

They left Belle and Jock with Mr. MacKenzie.

"I'll be keeping them in the wee paddock," Mr. MacKenzie told them. "And I'll be leaving Betsy off her chain tonight, just in case there's any sign of your friends."

"Has Miss Tuke phoned?" Jinny demanded, as soon as she got into the kitchen.

"Yes," said Mrs. Manders. "Dad spoke to her. She went with the policeman to the tinkers' camp this morning, but they found nothing. No trace of anything suspicious, and naturally all the tinkers swore they hadn't been away from the camp last night."

"What's she going to do now?" asked Jinny.

"Advertise," said her mother. "She's including Bramble and Shantih in the advertisement. The police have circulated descriptions of them all and they'll be on the lookout at any horse sales and slaughterhouses."

Diving from the kitchen, Jinny just made the bathroom before she was sick.

By half-past ten, Ken still hadn't returned.

"He said he might not be back," said Mrs. Manders. "You'll see him tomorrow. No point in staying up any later or you'll be too tired to do anything tomorrow."

Reluctantly, Jinny agreed. Sue had gone to bed at nine, saying that if she stayed up any longer her face would split with yawning. She was fast asleep when Jinny went into their bedroom.

Jinny sat down on the edge of her bed—elbows on her knees, head buried in her hands. The day's happenings unrolled like a newsreel behind her eyes, from the first moment when she had discovered the empty field, to the hopeless, leaden despair that weighed her down as she sat listening for the sound of Nell Storr's car that would bring Ken home.

It was after midnight before Jinny gave up. She undressed, crawled into bed and, pulling the bedclothes over her head, cried in silent misery. It was all too terrible, too terrible to have happened. Although Jinny's brain knew that it had happened she could not make herself believe it.

CHAPTER SEVEN

"Miss Tuke is positive the tinkers have taken them?" asked Ken.

Jinny nodded. "She's sure."

Ken had got home in the early morning. He'd read a note from Mr. Manders telling him what had happened, and woken Jinny. They were sitting in the dawn-bleak kitchen and Ken, having listened to Jinny's account of yesterday, was trying to think where they should look today.

"Do you think it was them?" Ken asked.

Jinny considered. "Might be. They're the most suspicious," she said.

"Not very likely," said Ken. "They've only just arrived, got work and a camp site. If they were going to steal horses they'd wait until they were ready to move on, wouldn't they?"

"Then who?"

"We don't know, but the tinkers will. There hasn't been

horse stealing going on more or less next door to their camp without them knowing about it."

"Why didn't they tell Miss Tuke if they knew?"

"Would you have told her if you'd been a tinker? You'd have kept your mouth shut. They wouldn't want to tell the police anything, but if you rode over you might be able to find out something. Try to blend in so they stop noticing you. See everything without staring at anything."

"We'll go this morning," agreed Jinny. She was rather vague about what Ken thought they should do, but it seemed as good an idea as any to have a look at the tinkers' camp herself.

"I'll go over to Ardtallon," said Ken. "A word here and a word there. See what's blowing."

He uncurled his long legs from under the kitchen table, stretched, then, soft footed as a cat, walked out of the kitchen. Minutes later, Jinny heard the front door closing gently behind him.

Jinny's father wasn't too keen on them visiting the tinkers' camp by themselves.

"I could drive you over in the afternoon," he offered.

"But we want to ride," Jinny said. "After all, Sue is here on holiday and we'd rather go by ourselves."

"Well, be sensible. Don't do anything crazy. If the police and Miss Tuke couldn't find anything, there's nothing there to be found."

Jock and Belle were difficult to catch. Even in Mr. MacKenzie's small paddock they managed to avoid capture until Mr. MacKenzie came out with a scoop of oats. He stayed to help them tack up the ponies, heaving up the stiff canvas girths and giving Jinny directions on how to reach Alec McGowan's farm.

"You'll find the tinks camping down by the river. Be taking a care for them now. Don't you be pushing your noses in where they're not wanted. If you see Alec McGowan, be telling him I'll be at the market next month."

"Will do," promised Jinny, her heels thwacking into Jock's sides, her riding stick battering against his hairy quarters as she tried to ride him out of the yard.

"Now they're trotting don't let them stop," Jinny warned Sue. "Keep them moving."

"My bum's numb," moaned Sue. "This saddle is made out of cast iron."

Suddenly the sound of approaching hooves made the Highlands dig in their toes in an emergency stop. Clutching handfuls of mane, Jinny just managed to wriggle back into the saddle as Clare Burnley, riding Jasper, her black horse, trotted round the corner in front of them.

"Poor darlings!" she exclaimed, looking down on Sue and Jinny from the height of her thoroughbred. "I've heard all about it and it is too ghastly for words. Daddy has had alarms fitted on all our boxes and the tack room. Was she insured?"

Jinny stared blankly at Clare. She hadn't even known that you could insure horses.

"No? Lord, how foolish. I was saying to Ma that one would have rather a job getting the insurance to cough up before the Show, and if you did get the cash out of them, where would one look for another horse up here? But, of course, if you weren't insured . . ."

"We're going to find Shantih," Jinny told her.

"Oh, one would rather fear not. These gangs are so frightfully well organised. Has one any hope at all?"

Jinny gathered up Jock's reins and, her heels battering his sides, her stick bouncing off his coconut-fibre coat, she charged him into electronic speed and forced him past Clare.

"Steady on," exclaimed Clare, as Jasper shied. "No need to get into such a state. In fact, one would think that you'd be rather glad to have her taken off your hands. She does make such an utter fool of you in public."

"Seems a nice girl," said Sue, catching up with Jinny.

"One does always find her so utterly charming," Jinny replied, too worried about Shantih to be really annoyed by someone as rude as Clare.

Jock and Belle settled into a trot as heavy and steady as their walk.

"Clockwork," said Sue. "They're computerised."

"Silicon chip," said Jinny, her mind full of nothing but the thought of Shantih—the dreadful knowledge that every minute might be the minute when Shantih was being led into a slaughterhouse.

"They wouldn't sell an Arab for meat," she said to Sue, seeking reassurance. "They'd get more money selling her, wouldn't they?"

"Dunno," said Sue. "They get so much for meat nowadays."

"Thanks very much," said Jinny.

"But probably an Arab would be different," Sue added hurriedly. "In fact, I'm sure it would be."

"Don't bother," said Jinny. "You told me the first time."

When they reached the forestry track that led to Miss Tuke's, they kicked the Highlands into a gallumphing canter.

"Left here," said Jinny, when at last they reached the turn-off that Mr. MacKenzie had told her about. "Through this gate," she added, letting Jock settle back into plod.

"What shall we say?" asked Sue, as they rode up a field and Mr. McGowan's farmhouse came into sight. "Are we going to mention the horses?"

"Not if we can help it," said Jinny, as they rode down to the river. "Ken said we were to try not to be noticed, but I don't see how we can manage that. They're bound to notice us."

"Play it by ear," said Sue, without much conviction.

"More or less what Ken meant" Jinny agreed.

The tinkers were camped in a shingly swerve of the river bank. A track led from their camp over the fields in the direction of the farm. Two battered vans were parked on the track, and the camp itself looked like a mound of ancient tarpaulins with a tin chimney stuck on top of the mound—as if someone had picked a giant black mushroom, put it on the ground and stuck its stalk on top of it.

As they approached, a young woman who had been sitting on the ground by the fire stood up, shouted something, and two teenage boys came out of the tarpaulin mound and stood staring at them. Three ragged-looking terriers, bouncing and yapping, came scrabbling towards them.

"What are we going to say?" insisted Sue, her voice squeaky with nerves.

Jinny didn't know and didn't care. The tinkers were her only link with Shantih. There must be some way she could find out what they knew.

An old woman with grey hair hanging about her face came out of one of the vans, joined the younger woman, and they both stood staring as Jinny and Sue rode up.

"Would you be wanting to buy a flower from the tinker folk?" whined the old woman, holding out a large wicker basket filled with flowers made from wood chips, and small wicker plant pots. "Buy a flower." She stretched out a claw-like hand and gripped Jinny's knee.

"They're lovely flowers," said Jinny. "Did you make them yourself?"

"I did. You'll not be knowing the work of the tinkers, grand folk like yourselves."

Five or six ragged children had come out of the vans and were staring up at Jinny and Sue with pale, closed faces.

"We don't have any money with us," Jinny said. "Or we would like to buy some. We might come back and buy some now that we've seen them."

"Be doing that," said the old woman, tightening her grip for a second before she took her hand off Jinny's knee.

"If you've not the money to buy anything you'll be riding on then," said the young woman. The menace in her voice was October ice on water.

There was a silence when Jinny couldn't think of a thing to say—a silence that grew tighter as the dark eyes of the tinkers stared up at them, devouring, without expression.

"I must ask them if they've seen Shantih," Jinny thought, but she knew it would be useless. If she asked directly, they would tell her nothing. But she had to ask. Had to find out. She couldn't ride off without asking. Then, suddenly, she knew what to say.

"Really we came to see how the dog is. We're the girls that took your dog to the vet after the float hit him."

The younger woman's face relaxed into a slow smile. She spoke in a low voice to the older woman and the boys, and the tension had gone. The old woman urged them to take their pick of her flowers, the two boys praised Jock and Belle, and the young woman said they must stay until Tam came back. He was out with his father and the dogs, but they would be back in a moment and they would see for themselves how well the dog's leg was healing.

Jinny and Sue dismounted. Their arms through their reins, they picked flowers from the woman's basket while the children hoisted each other on to the ponies' backs. The young woman piled sticks on the fire, flames leapt up round the soot-black kettle.

Jinny imagined what it would be like to live with the tinkers. Not to live in a house, but to live outside. Not to think about keeping clean, or being polite, or caring what other people thought about you. Knowing always that they were suspicious of everything you did and didn't want you near them. Jinny saw herself sitting round the fire at night; waking outdoors on a summer morning; selling wooden flowers around the villages, basket over her arm, riding bareback on Shantih.

"Shantih!" the word turned like a knife in Jinny's heart. She looked carefully round the camp but there was no sign of halters or any other tack. No sign of horses.

"Do you have any ponies of your own?" Jinny asked one of the boys.

"Aye, times," said the boy.

Suddenly the terriers burst into a flurry of yapping. Over the track from the farm came two figures—a man and a boy. Two brindled lurchers, one with a hind leg tucked close to its body, ran in front of them.

"Tam's coming now," said the young woman. "It's Jake himself will be wanting to thank you for your kindness."

As the man and the boy came closer, Jinny saw that Jake was the same man who had been on Miss Tuke's hill, the same man who had stood silent and dark in the shadow of the pines and stared after them when they had ridden past —when she had been riding Shantih.

The boy, Tam, ran with the lurchers, and when he reached Jinny and Sue he gripped his dog by the scruff of its neck and pulled him over so that Jinny and Sue could see his injured leg.

"He's still fit for the rabbits," he said, beaming at them.

"Oh good," said Jinny.

"It does seem to be healing," said Sue, as Jake came striding up, kicking the boy and the dog out of his way.

"Get out of here," he said in a low snarl.

"Jake," said the young woman. "What's at you? That's the lassies who took the dog to be stitched. We've them to thank . . ."

"Get away from here," Jake roared, his face livid, his lips drawn back from his lower teeth, his eyes narrow slits.

"We only came to see how the dog was," exclaimed Jinny.

"It was the two of you who were on the hill with that Tuke woman, and her bringing the police to snoop around my camp. Get out with you both."

The smell of spirits reeked from the man's breath.

"Jake, man, you're wandered. It's the lassies had the dog stitched up," said the young woman.

Jake spun round on her. Jinny saw his clenched fist aimed at her head, saw her shield her face with the same movement that the boy had used to protect himself when Jinny had spoken to him at the gymkhana. Jinny shut her eyes, heard the blow hit the woman, and opened her eyes to see her fall to the ground, her mouth bleeding.

"Get off with you," roared Jake, advancing on them.

Sue and Jinny were on their ponies and up the track almost before they knew what they were doing.

"But I didn't ask him," cried Jinny. "I didn't ask about Shantih." And she pulled Jock round and forced him back to the tinkers' camp.

"I didn't come to snoop," Jinny yelled. "I came to see if you knew anything about Shantih? She's my horse, a chestnut Arab, and she's been stolen. Do you know anything about her? Tell me. You must tell me if you know. Please! Please!"

For a moment the man stood without speaking, then he gave a low whistle and the two lurchers sprang at Jinny. Jock, from a dim, wolf-haunted past, squealed a high, pig squeal, half reared and lashed at the dogs with his forelegs before he spun round and went galloping back to Sue and Belle.

Before they reached Sue, Jake had called his dogs off.

"Come on," said Sue, urging Belle on. "No more of this. Pippen needs me."

"But they must know something. They must know, or they wouldn't have been so mad at finding us there. They know where Shantih is. They know where the ponies are."

"We're not going back," stated Sue. "He'd kill us, and he'd never tell you."

"We could search for them."

"Look," said Sue. "The police and Miss Tuke were here. They had a warrant to search the place. They didn't find anything. What makes you think we would?"

Jinny didn't answer, but rode on unwillingly with Sue. They went through Mr. McGowan's farmyard and down a lane leading away from the farm.

Jock stopped—legs foursquare, head high.

"Whatever now?" growled Jinny.

There was something coming towards them, something scrabbling along the ditch at the bottom of the hawthorn hedge.

Coated with mud, dead leaves and twigs, the tinker boy, Tam, crawled out of the ditch at their side. For a moment he stood with his head cocked to one side, listening.

"Do you know where Shantih and Bramble are?" demanded Jinny. "Tell us if you know. You must tell us."

Tam paid no attention to her urgent questions. He was like a wild creature that any second would plunge away and vanish.

"They're up there," Tam said in a low whisper, and he pointed to a track that led over a hillside in the middle distance. "They took them up there."

Jinny and Sue looked where the boy was pointing.

"Where could you hide ponies up there?" asked Sue suspiciously.

"Up in the Barony," muttered the boy. "Aye."

They stared up at where the boy had pointed.

"How do we get there?" demanded Jinny. "How far is it?"

But when she looked down, the boy had gone.

CHAPTER EIGHT

"He's vanished!" exclaimed Sue, unable to believe her eyes.

"He can't have," said Jinny. "He's got to tell us more."

She stared urgently up and down the lane. Standing in her stirrups she peered over the hedge, then rode up and down the lane shouting for Tam, but there was no sign of him.

Eventually Jinny caught a fleeting glimpse of him, almost out of sight. He was running full pelt, low to the ground, heading back to the tinkers' camp.

"No point in following him," Jinny said. "We'll not get anything more out of him."

"Do you think he really knows where they are? He might be making it up."

"Of course he does. He only risked coming to tell us because we had his dog stitched up for him. Jake would murder him if he knew. He wouldn't have come to tell us unless he was really sure."

"We can't reach that track from here," said Sue, for although they could see the track stretching across the next range of hills, there seemed no way of getting to it.

"Better ask at the farm," said Jinny. "We'll give them Mr. MacKenzie's message."

The farmer's wife opened the door.

"Morning," said Jinny. "We've brought a message from Mr. MacKenzie of Finmory Farm. He told us to let you know that he would be at the market next month."

"Och now, Alec will be pleased to hear that. I'll be letting him know. That'll be Ewan's ponies you're riding?"

"They are," said Jinny. "We're having a day's trek. Mr. MacKenzie suggested we should ride to the Barony, but we seem to have gone wrong."

"Aye," said Mrs. McGowan. "You'll need to go out on to the road again, go back the way you came and watch out for a gate. You'll see it easily enough. The fine broad track it was once when they still farmed the Barony, though that will not be yesterday, more's the pity."

"Is it a farm?" asked Sue.

"Och, it's nothing but an old ruin now, but once it was a bonnie wee bit farm."

"Do we follow the track all the way?" Jinny asked impatiently.

"Aye, to the very door. I daresay it's overgrown a wee bit nowadays. If it's used once a year it would be surprising me. But you'd best be getting on with you, for it's a fair step up to the Barony."

"Thanks," said Jinny, urging Jock forward. "Thanks a lot."

At a steady trot they rode back down the lane, turned right and rode on, keeping a look-out for the gate. They saw it at last—a rickety bundle of lichen-covered timber, tied to the gatepost by wire.

Jinny jumped down, untwisted the wire and lifted back the gate.

"She was right," said Sue. "No one ever comes through here. That gate's had it."

"Yet the wire's new. You'd think it would be rusty but it's not. There's the old bit. Look, someone's chucked it in the hedge and fitted this new bit round the gate."

"And wheel marks," said Sue, pointing to the soft ground at the side of the gatepost. "Someone's driven through here and not long ago, I'd say."

Jinny struggled to drag the gate back, retwisted the wire and sprang back up on to Jock.

"Come on!" Jinny yelled, as she kicked him into a heavy, thumping canter.

As they followed the track over the hills, Jinny refused to allow herself to think that they had found Shantih and Bramble, that it was possible that they were at the ruined farm.

"Don't think it," she warned herself. "It may be other ponies Tam saw. Some farmer may be grazing his ponies up there. They may not be stolen ponies at all. It may not be Shantih." But the leaden weight that had been choking her since she had first discovered the empty field had gone.

Jock and Belle had slowed to a walk that, despite all efforts, was rapidly slowing to a plod.

"Miles," said Sue. "It must be right in the hills."

Looking back, Jinny could see McGowan's farm as a tiny, toy building, the loops of the river drawn on to the fields by a child's paintbrush and the tinkers' camp a hardly visible mound by the river bank. She shivered, thinking for the first time of what they would do if Jake was sitting waiting for them—a giant spider in his web of crumbling walls. Jinny longed for Shantih's speed. If she had been riding Shantih she would have been safe, for no one could have caught her then.

"Have you decided what we are actually going to do when we get there?" asked Sue.

"Spy out the place," said Jinny vaguely. She had only thought of seeing Shantih again, of knowing she was safe.

"Can't spy when we're riding these two," said Sue. "They'll hear us coming."

As she spoke, they rounded a corner of the track and the old farmhouse lay in a hollow in front of them.

"Quick," said Jinny, "back out of sight in case there's a lookout."

"Should we just ride up?" suggested Sue, when they were both safely round the corner again. "All we can do just now is look for the horses. Make sure they are here, then ride back and tell the police."

"No," said Jinny. "If they are here we've got to set them free. Once they're loose on the moors they'll be safe. They'll find their own way home."

"But if we set them free what will happen to us?" said Sue. "Don't think whoever has stolen them is going to stand there and say thank you."

"Don't care," said Jinny. "As long as Shantih and Bramble are O.K. They won't slaughter us."

"That's daft," said Sue.

"You'd be the same if it was Pippen."

Sue didn't reply, and for a minute they sat astride their ponies staring at each other.

"I'm going," said Jinny, jumping to the ground and tossing Jock's reins to Sue.

"But . . ." began Sue.

"Makes sense," said Jinny. "They're not so likely to see one of us, and if they do catch me you can ride for help."

"Wait, I'll go," Sue said, but Jinny was already walking quickly round the corner.

There were no windows facing the track, only the crumbling wall of a building that looked as if it had once been a byre. Jinny searched for any sign of life, but all she could see were a few black-faced sheep.

"Nothing disturbing them," Jinny thought, and began to walk on towards the farm. "I'll tell them I'm a Girl Guide," she decided. "That I'm doing my Rambler's badge, that I've got lost. Wonder if I should be wearing a uniform?"

Jinny wasn't sure, but knowing a Guide wouldn't be wearing a hard hat she left it with her stick by the side of the track.

Just on the borders of Jinny's mind was the vision of Shantih; of how she was there only a few minutes away; of how she would look up, knowing Jinny; would whinny a welcome and come cantering to meet her. The picture was so clear that it was almost real. Jinny could see Shantih's dished face, wide eyes and velvet muzzle. Almost, Jinny could feel Shantih's hard neck and her silken fringe of mane. But it was not real. It had not happened. Not yet. Jinny pushed the dream out of her head.

She crept up to the wall, stood with her ears strained, listening for any sound that might be men or horses. Placing each foot gently down on the wrack of dead nettles and weeds, Jinny made her way along the wall. She peered round the end of the wall into the skeleton of what had once been the byre. At one end, milk churns and dairy pails lay in a confused, rusting litter. Down the sides of the byre Jinny could still make out where the cattle had stood, their troughs silted under a debris of dirt.

At the far side of the byre, a door that seemed to lead into the farmhouse kitchen stood half-open.

Jinny dug her nails into the palms of her hands and, breathing slowly, climbed over the rubble of the wall and crept across the byre. She waited by the door but still there was no sound. Inching forward, Jinny peered round the door into a stone-floored kitchen.

At first glance, Jinny saw only the sagging ceiling, cob-webbed walls and old sacks stuffed into broken window-panes. Then she took in the crushed beer cans littering the floor, a table made from milk crates and an old bench that had been brought in from outside. The fireplace of the range was full of fresh ashes and littered with cigarette ends. But the room was empty. No one was there now.

Jinny ran across the kitchen, opened the back door of the farm and stepped out into the yard. Its soft mud was scored with wheel tracks and hoofprints. The doors of a high, corrugated shed were wide open and the hoofprints seemed to come from inside the shed. Jinny dashed across. Peering into the half-dark, she saw that the floor of mud and decaying timbers was pitted with hoofprints and thick with dung. The smell of horses was heavy in the air.

Jinny stood quite still. Caught on a nail in the corrugated iron were several long chestnut hairs. They were Shantih's. Shantih had been here but they had taken her away again. Jinny was too late.

Jinny turned blindly into the yard. The weight was back in her chest, squeezing the breath out of her lungs so that she had to snatch for air. Where would she look now? Where? They had driven the horses away. If they had left last night they could be anywhere by now. Jinny imagined Shantih and Bramble crammed into a cattle float, standing terrified as they were driven through the dark. She could not imagine the men who had stolen them, men who would take a horse from its own field as if it were a pound of butter in a supermarket, who could steal a living animal as if it were an object.

"Please God," breathed Jinny. "Please God."

Sue, riding to meet Jinny, knew from her face that she hadn't found the ponies or Shantih.

"We're too late," Jinny told her. "They've been there but they've taken them away again. There's nothing we can do."

"For goodness sake," said Sue, "of course there must be something. Did you search the place? Look for clues. There must be something to tell us where they've gone."

They rode back to the farm, tied the ponies up and went into the kitchen. Sue looked round the room in disgust.

"What a filthy mess," she said, pushing the door wide open to let in more light.

"Bus tickets, cigarette packets, paper bags with the shop's address on them," said Sue, searching about. "Anything at all that might tell us where they've come from."

"Doesn't mean they'll be going back there," said Jinny despondently.

She wandered through the rest of the deserted farmhouse, but there was only dirt and decay. The staircase grinned with gap teeth where stairs had fallen in, the bannisters had been chopped down and carried off. All the other rooms except the kitchen were open to the sky.

"Not a thing," said Jinny, crossing the kitchen and going out into the yard.

She stood staring at the shed doorway, trying to picture Shantih and Bramble being led through it. Then something caught her eye. On a rotting water butt at the farm door there lay a copy of *Horse and Hound*. Someone had put it down and forgotten to lift it. Jinny picked it up. It was last week's issue. One of the horse thieves must have put it there and forgotten about it.

82

"This proves it wasn't the tinkers," Jinny said, showing it to Sue. "They'd never buy *Horse and Hound*."

"No name or delivery address on it?" questioned Sue.

"Not a scribble," said Jinny, examining the cover.

She flicked through the pages. Show horses and ponies stood in ribboned splendour, an Arab head tore at Jinny's heart, elegant men and women advertised expensive horsy clothing. There were advertisements at the end of the magazine—horses for sale, jobs vacant and future shows. Almost on the last page someone had doodled round one of the announcements, making a frame of heavy biro lines.

"Whareton Horse Sale," read Jinny. "Largest Horse Sale of the North. Whareton Sale Ground. Thursday, April 20th. Commences 10.00 a.m."

"Sue, listen!" Jinny screamed, and read the sale announcement out to Sue. "That's this Thursday. Not tomorrow but the next day. Look, they've marked it out specially."

Sue snatched the magazine from Jinny. "Yes!" she shouted. "Yes! That's it. That's where they're taking them."

"Must be," declared Jinny. "Must be. Look at the size of it. 'Over two hundred and eighty horses and ponies.' They'd think that no one would ever find stolen animals amongst that lot."

"Bet that's where they've taken them," said Sue.

"Come on," urged Jinny. "We've got to phone Miss Tuke."

"We've got to get there," Jinny said, as they hustled the ponies back down the track. "We must be there."

"If Miss Tuke won't go, will your dad take us?" asked Sue.

"Might," said Jinny. "If he won't, we'll go by train. I've got enough money for fares in my box."

"How will we get them home?"

"Take bridles," said Jinny. "Ride them home."

"But what about . . ." began Sue, then stopped.

Jinny didn't ask her what she had been going to say. For a second it had all seemed possible. The chance of finding the *Horse and Hound* had been so lucky that she had dismissed the necessity of getting to Whareton, the impossibility of finding Shantih and Bramble amongst so many horses.

"We will get there," she said to Sue. "We will find them. We MUST."

CHAPTER NINE

"I'll come round right away," Miss Tuke said, when Jinny phoned her. "Get all the gen." And in no time Miss Tuke's Pine Trekking Centre van was parked outside Finmory and Miss Tuke was inside, drinking coffee and listening intently to Sue and Jinny.

"First things first. Have you phoned the police?"

Mr. Manders said he had and that they were going up to Barony Farm first thing the next morning.

"Excellent," said Miss Tuke. "I'll phone when I get back home. Must link up with the police at Whareton Sale. Have our work cut out trying to track them down at that rodeo."

"You mean you'll take us? You'll go?" demanded Jinny.

Although it was still only the early evening, the one thing Jinny wanted to do was sleep. She hadn't even had enough energy left to think about how they would get to Whareton if Miss Tuke hadn't wanted to go to the sale.

"Take my horsebox," said Miss Tuke. "Bring the four of them home in that. *If* we find them. Who's coming? Jinny? Sue? How about a man? Might need some brawn. Mr. Manders?"

"Can't possibly. I've an article to write for Monday. It must be posted by Friday and I haven't even started it."

"Ken?" asked Jinny.

Ken was sitting on the floor, Kelly stretched beside him.

"Me? Go to a horse sale?" he asked incredulously. "I would go frantic!" And he waved his arms, windmill about

84

his head, fighting off the imagined horrors of the place. "No way."

"Please," said Jinny. "To find Shantih and Bramble. Please." But Ken didn't answer.

Jinny was too weary to argue and Miss Tuke had already abandoned the idea.

"I'll be over tomorrow night about ten. Must trek tomorrow. Arranged for the trekkers to be Inverburgh shoppers on Thursday. We'll drive by night. Reach Whareton sevenish. Give us time for breakfast and be in plenty of time for the sale."

Miss Tuke stood up, slapping her hands, palm down, on to the table.

"We'll show them," she said. "Whoever they are they won't get away with this."

As Miss Tuke passed behind Jinny's chair she clapped her hand on Jinny's shoulder. "Don't forget that mad creature's bridle. Don't want you being dragged round a horse sale trying to control her in a halter."

Jinny tried to smile, knew that Miss Tuke was being optimistic to make her feel better, but her face wouldn't move. It was as if her muscles weren't strong enough, had suddenly grown too tired, as if all her energy was being used up to keep her acting in the same way as other people, to stop her running madly round the house screaming, crying out that they must find Shantih and Bramble and bring them home, that they couldn't go on being polite and ordinary when something as terrible as this had happened.

"I won't forget," said Jinny.

"Well done," said Miss Tuke. "That's the spirit. Warm clothes and flasks. Be ready."

Although Jinny had felt so tired, when she did get to bed she couldn't sleep. She lay talking to Sue until Sue's answers became more and more drowsy and eventually stopped altogether.

Still Jinny couldn't sleep. She heard her parents and Ken going to bed and then the house settling into silence. She counted to one hundred and then back to one, but still there was nothing in her mind but the misery of Shantih gone "and no more mine."

"Where is she now?" Jinny thought wretchedly. "Now, this very minute?" And because the worst was possible— that already she might have been slaughtered—the best was possible too—that Shantih might have kicked her way to freedom and found her way back to Finmory, might be standing at the field gate waiting.

Jinny jumped out of bed and looked out. There was just enough moonlight to be certain that Shantih was not there.

Jinny turned and padded through to the other half of her bedroom. She stood in front of the mural of the Red Horse. It seemed to glow in the darkness, its yellow eyes blazing as it charged from the wall through the painted blue-green branches and the heavy-petalled flowers.

Although she knew it was only a painting, there was a part of Jinny that was afraid of the Horse. The dark, secret part of Jinny that she kept battened down, knew the Horse as a magic power. Now, in the darkness, it pushed up into Jinny's consciousness and because it was night-time she held out her hands to the Horse and whispered Shantih's name.

"Shantih," she mouthed, "Shantih," over and over again as if it was a spell or an incantation.

Jinny did not know how long she stood there, but when at last she stopped repeating the name she knew that Ken must come with them to Whareton Sale. If Ken did not come, they would not find Shantih.

Miss Tuke phoned before breakfast to tell Jinny to be sure to bring her insurance certificate with her.

"I'll bring Bramble's. Proof of ownership might be necessary."

"She's not insured," said Jinny.

"Predictable," said Miss Tuke. "Then go over to the vet's this morning and get him to sign a description of Shantih, stating that he's willing to identify her if necessary."

Sue and Jinny rode over to the vet's.

"I'd know her all right," he assured them, as he signed Jinny's description. "This to prove ownership? Miss Tuke should have no trouble. Most of hers are marked. One you have, the black Highland, he's got a nick in his right ear. That'll be noted on her insurance."

"That's right, he has," said Jinny. "I just thought it was where he had cut himself at some time."

The afternoon was endless. Jinny suffocated under minutes as long as hours.

"We should be doing something NOW," she nagged at Sue, who was reading.

"Nothing we can do," said Sue, not lifting her head.

Restlessly, Jinny went to look for Ken but couldn't find him. She trailed up to her bedroom to stand in front of the Red Horse, but by day it was only a painting and could tell her nothing.

Jinny sat on her windowsill, staring out at the empty field, at the sea, shades of amethyst under the clear spring sky. Sometimes in her imagination she walked into the sale to find Shantih straight away, standing tied in a row of horses, turning to whinny as she recognised Jinny; and Bramble, glowering to himself under his forelock, furious that any self-respecting trekking pony should have been treated in this way. And sometimes they were driving back to Finmory, the horsebox empty and rattling. How would that be? Where would she look next? What would she do then?

"If Ken doesn't come, I won't find her," thought Jinny. "He must come," and she went back to searching for him.

At last she found him working in the kitchen garden.

"I've been looking for you everywhere," declared Jinny. "Where have you been?"

"Here and there," said Ken vaguely.

"You will come with us to the sale, won't you? It's to find Shantih. If you don't come, I'm sure we won't find her. Miss Tuke's O.K. but she's not like you. She'll organise things, but you'd look. If Shantih and Bramble are there, you'd find them."

Ken lent on his fork, staring into the distance.

"It will be like torture for me," he said. "Terrified animals. Men shouting, hitting them. Horses that have

worked all their lives for humans, chucked out like gar-
bage."

"It's to find Shantih and Bramble. To save them. It's for
them. And some of the horses that are there will be going to
good homes."

"If you cared even that for an animal," said Ken, snapping his fingers, "would you send it to a sale? They're wild,
free creatures and we've taken them and nailed metal to
their feet and put metal in their mouths. They are all
created wind-swift and beautiful. What would it be like, a
true sharing between men and horses? And look what we
do to them."

"I know," said Jinny. "I do know and I want it to be like
that too—riding bareback without bridles, only love. But
it's not like that. Shantih's real and it's the real Shantih I
love. That's why I've got to go to this sale and find her. If
you come, we'll find her. I asked the Red Horse and you
must come with us."

Never in a hundred years would Jinny have told anyone
else but Ken about the Red Horse, but she knew that he
would understand.

"I'll come," said Ken. "I would have come anyway. It's
just that when something like this comes up, I always try
to find ways round it, ways out. Really, I'm soft through
and through," and he smiled in self-mockery. "We'll find
them. Let us cultivate our little gardens." And Ken went
on digging.

Mrs. Manders had made a special evening meal, but
there was only Jinny and Sue to share it with her. Mike was
at Ardtallon at a football match, Mr. Manders was writing,
and Ken was eating his usual meal of brown rice and vegetables.

"Look at it this way," Mrs. Manders said, trying to cheer
Jinny up a little. "If you hadn't found the *Horse and
Hound* with the sale marked in it, you would be sitting here
with absolutely no idea of where to look for them. At least
this way you can do something positive."

"It's no use," said Jinny, pushing away the plate of her
favourite chocolate peppermint ice cream. "I can't eat any

more. I know you're right and that's sensible, but it's not the way I feel."

Tears were hot behind her eyes and she got up quickly and ran out of the room.

"I'd be just the same if it was Pippen," Sue said. Ever since Shantih and Bramble had been stolen she had been making nightly reverse-charge phone calls to check that Pippen was recovering satisfactorily from his warble, but really to know that he was safe. "If it was Pippen, I don't know what I'd do."

"What is Jinny going to do if she doesn't find her at this sale?" said Mrs. Manders.

Miss Tuke arrived shortly after ten. She refused coffee and bustled Sue, Jinny, Ken and Kelly into the cabin of her horsebox. Sue had a shopper with four flasks in it, two with soup and two with coffee, and several bags of Mrs. Manders' sandwiches and baking.

"Glad to see we won't starve," beamed Miss Tuke.

Jinny had two halters and Shantih's bridle. It had been almost dark when she had at last forced herself to go down to the stables to fetch them. It had felt strange, taking Shantih's bridle from its hook, as if it were an action that had once been familiar and that she hadn't done for years. Yet it was only three days since she had last ridden Shantih; four days since the gymkhana, when all that had mattered had been to win the cup. Jinny had hurried out of the stables not looking at the empty box, slamming the door behind her, shuddering as she tore up the path back to the security of the house.

"Phone us whenever you find them," Mr. Manders said, waving goodbye.

"We'll be thinking about you all the time," Mrs. Manders called. "Good luck. I'm sure you'll find them."

Spinning round in a ferocious U-turn, Miss Tuke drove the box down the drive.

"Map in the door pocket," she said. "Navigators all of you. Can't expect me to drive and map read."

The horsebox bounced along the narrow country roads, its headlights slashing swathes of silhouetted hedgerows and frantic glimpses of trees lit from beneath, that rose out of the blackness and fell away almost before Jinny's eyes could focus on them. It was an unending kaleidoscope of electric colour. Gradually the twisting leafy roads gave way to broader roads that looped over rolling hills.

"Be on the motorway soon," Miss Tuke said. "Stop for a bite of grub before that."

Squashed in the cabin they shared soup and rolls and apple pie.

"Straight on to Whareton," Miss Tuke announced, as they drove on to the motorway.

At first, Jinny tried to keep awake, gripped by the phantasmagoria of motorway signs that sprang at them from the darkness like weird electronic ghouls on a ghost-train ride. Cars and coaches zoomed past them, zombies crouched over steering wheels, whey-faced passengers staring out from their glass cages. All bound on desperation errands they hurtled through the night.

Kelly and Sue were fast asleep. Ken stared, glaze-eyed, straight ahead. Miss Tuke swore at other drivers and Jinny fought to stay awake, to experience the force and power of this unknown night world. But in spite of herself, her eyes closed, her head dropped heavily on to her chest and she slept.

"Stopping here for the loo," roused Miss Tuke. "Then coffee."

Jinny jerked awake from a dream of Shantih, fumbled out of the cabin more than half asleep.

Back in the box she clutched her mug of steaming coffee in both hands. Her teeth chattered. She was drawn tight and shivering into the clenched centre of herself, was glad of the warm crush of bodies in the cabin, glad of Miss Tuke's bouncy self-confidence. She stared out at the brilliantly-lit concrete-and-glass, science-fiction structure of the service point where they had stopped, and shivered uncontrollably. Ken put his arm, tight and strong, round her shoulders.

"It's a nightmare," he whispered. "See it for the dream it is. Be without fear."

"Four hours more and we'll be there," announced Miss Tuke, stabbing the map with her blunt forefinger. "We'll contact the police whenever we arrive. They'll know about us."

The next time Jinny woke, the motorway was bordered by rows of red-brick houses and brick-edged patches of garden. The morning sky was aflame with scarlet and sun-gold clouds.

They drove through the empty streets of Whareton and stopped for breakfast at an all-night café.

"Straight on here, right, second left at traffic lights, then on until we see the sale ground," Miss Tuke said, repeating the directions the waitress had given them.

Above the high, wrought-iron gates set in the blank, whitewashed wall, Jinny read the giant letters of WHARETON SALE GROUNDS. Somehow the night had brought her from Finmory to here. Had Shantih and Bramble travelled the same road? Or were they still on the road, swaying to the movements of the box that was bringing them to the sale?

Jinny forced all doubt from her mind. Ken had come with them. They would find Shantih.

CHAPTER TEN

Miss Tuke followed the arrows that pointed the way to where the horseboxes were to be parked. She drove into a large, gravelled parking area. Already horseboxes and floats were fringing the space. Two bay ponies were tied up outside one of the boxes. A man led a black thoroughbred out of a trailer and across the parking space. It reared up, striking out against the grey city sky. Three children with riding crops and noise tried to persuade a stubborn pony to leave its box and risk the perilous journey down the ramp. Anticipation tingled in the air.

"Sale starts at ten," said Miss Tuke. "We'll each get a sale catalogue. Jinny and I will go to see the auctioneers and the police. Ken and Sue, split up. Look around. Remember they may have changed the ponies' appearance. Bramble has a nick, halfway down the inside of his right ear. My two are mouse duns—mouse colour with darker manes and tails. They've feathers at their heels, but they may have been clipped. Moll is 13.2, Polly slightly higher. Both galled on their front legs. Farmer I bought them from used to hobble them. Shouldn't think they could disguise that."

Jinny tried to concentrate on what Miss Tuke was saying, knowing it was important, but she could hardly stand still for her eagerness to be in the sale ground. Her eyes checked on every least movement in case it should be Shantih.

"Meet back here at a quarter to ten," finished Miss Tuke. "We'll arrange a rota for watching the sale ring." And she marched into the sale ground, Jinny trotting at her side.

Most of the sale ground was divided into pens by metal bars, and, to Jinny's surprise, many of the pens already had ponies in them. Some were filled with a mass of youngsters, packed in so closely that heads rested on other pony's necks and on rumps still fluffy with their baby coats. Their eyes were staring, their nostrils wide, their ears trembling to the sights and sounds of this alien place. Numbers were pasted on their rumps.

"Scrub," said Miss Tuke. "Been here all night."

For a moment, Jinny allowed herself to see it as Ken would see it. Saw the snatches of fern and grasses in the ponies' manes and tails and knew that they must have been separated from their herd, brought from open spaces to the waiting cattle float. She felt the terror of the journey to the sale, saw the stark panic in their eyes as they waited. She knew what Ken meant when he talked about the screaming of the animals.

"Don't," said Jinny to herself. "Don't see it. Don't let it get at you. You're here to find Shantih. There's nothing you can do. Horse sales go on all the time. Slaughterhouses kill animals all the time, everyday. You're here to find Shantih and Bramble. That's what you're here for."

"Brisk up, Jennifer Manders," said Miss Tuke, as if she could read Jinny's thoughts.

Jinny pushed her long hair back from her face, squared her shoulders and shook the weariness of the night's journey out of her head.

"Right," she said. "I'm here."

They went first to the auctioneer's office where two young men were drinking tea and arranging papers.

"The police will have informed you about us," Miss Tuke told them. "We're down from Inverburgh. Chasing stolen horses. Tuke is the name. Three Highlands and one Arab. More or less certain they're here."

"You need to see Mr. Forrest, the auctioneer, ducks. He'll be here in half an hour."

"We'll be back," said Miss Tuke, and they went in search of a policeman.

The one they found was decidedly younger than the two men in the auctioneer's office. Miss Tuke regarded him with displeasure.

"Officer," she said, standing squarely in front of him. "I am Tuke. Miss Tuke . . ."

"Ah, good," said the policeman. "Stolen ponies, isn't it? Got the details here." He flicked open a notebook.

"And an Arab," said Jinny.

"Chestnut," read the policeman. "White face, four white stockings. Five/six years of age."

Jinny was speechless at such efficiency. For a moment it almost seemed as if the policeman would point to a horse-box, telling her that she would find Shantih inside it, but he only took his walkie-talkie out and called up two other policemen. When they arrived, one was comfortingly older than Miss Tuke.

"If you spot the horses, let us know. Don't do anything yourselves unless the situation is desperate, then be sure to send someone for us at once. We want you to get your horses back but we also want to catch the men who did it. Been getting away with far too much of this sort of thing.

Been a lot of it in the north, but if it's the same bunch, they've never been so far as Scotland before."

"Did you get the other horses back?" demanded Jinny. "The ones they stole before?"

"Don't you worry yourself about that," said the older policeman—adult speaking to child—"you enjoy yourself. Have a good day at the sale," so that Jinny's faith in him vanished.

"Should we find anything," continued the policeman to Miss Tuke, "we'll call you over the loudspeakers. We'll keep our eyes skinned and keep a watch on the meat men. They often buy up ponies before they get near the ring. Swop them from the box that brings them here into their own."

As the policemen left, the young man winked at Jinny, giving her the thumbs-up sign. Jinny grinned back, her eyes searching the sale ground for Ken.

They went back to the auctioneer's office and found Mr. Forrest, who was more interested in his sale than in stolen ponies.

"Shall we leave it in the hands of the police?" he said.

"Here are the details of the stolen ponies," said Miss Tuke, ignoring his suggestion.

"Two mouse-dun Highlands, one black Highland," said Mr. Forrest, reading Miss Tuke's list. "Common," he said. "Be about sixty Highlands here today. Check the catalogue for yourselves. No saying what colour yours will be by now. Chestnut Arab. Now we might notice her. Don't see them so often. A few here today."

"We'll be at the ringside," said Miss Tuke. "Might have to cause a disturbance. You'll know what's what." Then she stomped back out to the sale ground.

Everywhere that Jinny looked there were horses and ponies. Some were tied in rows to rings set in the walls, some jigsawed into the chequered pattern of pens now nearly all filled with animals.

Children climbed on the bars between the pens. Boys with sticks copied their elders, thumping and banging on unsuspecting rumps. Girls held out sweets. Men struggled to control fit horses excited by the noise and smells of the place. Women in headsquares, sheepskin jackets and boots led in native ponies. Horsy mothers walked beside children, demonstrating the patent safety qualities of the pony they had outgrown.

There were horses and ponies of every shape, size, type and temperament. Far, far more than Jinny had expected to find.

Jinny paused, staring round, wondering if any of the men who jostled about her might be the men who had stolen Shantih and Bramble, might be the dreaded meat men, for they must be there although there was nothing to distinguish them from any other person at the sale. Jinny longed to run wildly through the sale ground calling Shantih's name, searching until she found her.

"Catalogues," said Miss Tuke, looking at her watch. "Then back to the others. Don't wilt yet."

Ken and Kelly were waiting for them. Sue came running up minutes later.

"There are so many," she gasped. "Masses of Highlands, but I haven't seen any Arabs yet."

"We'll take it in turn to wait here," Miss Tuke said, leading the way to the entrance to the sale ring. "Best place. Spot them as they're waiting to come into the ring. Galls on the forelegs above the fetlock. Check every Highland in case they've been at them with a paint pot. You'll all know Bramble and Shantih. Anything remotely Brambleish, check his ear. Nick on the right ear. O.K.?"

They said it was.

"I'll take the first hour, then you lot come back here and we'll see how we're doing."

Ken's face was set into a hard mask—mouth clenched, eyes ablaze with disgust at all that he saw around him.

"I've started working my way round the pens," said Sue. "So I'll just go on. A lot of them have Highlands in them."

"I'm going to search for Arabs," said Jinny, ducking away from Ken. Having forced him to come, she felt too guilty to stay with him.

She hurried down the rows of tied horses, hope springing as she saw chestnut hocks and quarters; fading when a chestnut head with a Roman nose and piggy eyes looked round at her. Twice Jinny caught a glimpse of horses that for a rending second she thought must be Shantih, but when she got closer to them they were not anything like her.

The catalogue said there were six Arabs. Jinny found them all—one sorrel and five greys. Not one of them could possibly have been Shantih.

"Whoever stole them must have made their entries before they knew what horses they would be bringing," Jinny thought. "So probably Shantih won't be entered as an Arab. She'll be 'Lady's riding mare' or 'Well-mannered hack'."

"Will Miss Tuke come immediately to the main gates," boomed the loudspeaker. "Miss Tuke is wanted at the main gates."

Jinny froze, hardly able to believe her ears.

"It means they've found them," she cried to a complete stranger, before she ran, dodging and skipping through the crowd, towards the main gates.

"If Miss Tuke has left the ringside there's no one to watch the horses they're selling now," Jinny thought suddenly. "They may not have found them all. Shantih could be in the ring now and we'd miss her."

Jinny spun round and dashed to the sale ring. Ken was standing at the entrance.

"I'm here instead of Miss Tuke," he said.

"Shall I stay?"

Ken didn't answer, and after a minute Jinny decided that there was no point in both of them being there.

"I'll go and see what's happening," she said, not exactly speaking to Ken, rather announcing her departure.

There was only the young policeman at the gates.

"I heard you calling Miss Tuke," Jinny told him.

"We've got two of your horses," he said. "They're over by one of the pens." He pointed to where Jinny could just make out policemen's uniforms among the crowds.

"Only two," thought Jinny, as she raced across. "Oh, please God, let it be Shantih and Bramble. Let one of them be Shantih."

Miss Tuke was holding the halter ropes of two mouse-dun Highlands. It was Miss Tuke's ponies they had found. Jinny stopped dead in her tracks. Not Shantih, not Bramble, but two trekking ponies that Miss Tuke would sell tomorrow if she had a good enough offer for them.

"I found them," yelled Sue, sparkling with achievement. "I spotted their legs."

Jinny couldn't make herself speak.

"I know it's not Shantih," Sue added, seeing Jinny's face. "But it proves we're right. They have brought them here. The others must be here too. We'll find them next."

A white-haired man wearing a stockman's coat was standing between the two policemen, while Miss Tuke was showing them official-looking documents.

"States there under 'Distinguishing Features'—galled in both forlegs. Rest of the description fits to a T. Without a doubt, they are my beasts," she was saying.

"Ain't nothing to do with me," stated the white-haired man. "The gaffer tells me what horseflesh to bring here and I brings it. No questions. You can't pin nothing on me. Two carthorses and these two here. Picked them up in the yards this morning. Brought them in here now. You ain't got nothing on me. The gaffer's the one you want."

"We're quite satisfied that they're yours," one of the policemen said to Miss Tuke. "I'll keep the insurance certificates and we'll be in touch with you later."

"Is it in order to put them in my box? Take them back with us tonight?"

"Under the circumstances, quite in order. You won't be selling them before the whole matter is cleared up, will you? We may need you to give evidence if we can get a case together."

"Don't forget there's two more," said Jinny. "The Arab and the black Highland. You've got to find them as well."

"Eleven o'clock, miss, and fifty per cent of the stolen property returned. We'll sort out the rest before much longer."

"They seem none the worse for it," declared Miss Tuke, after she had examined her ponies. "Not starving, either," she said, when they had watered them and loaded them into the box and the ponies were nosing, without interest, at the armfuls of hay that Miss Tuke had just given to them.

"If only they could talk, they could tell us where they've been," said Jinny, a lump choking in her throat. It should have been Shantih and Bramble who were standing there. She knew she should have been glad that Miss Tuke had rescued her ponies, but she wasn't. It was Shantih and Bramble she wanted.

"Now, let's get on with it," said Miss Tuke, thumping her hand down on one of the solid rumps. "Ken's standing duty at the ringside. Help me get this ramp up and we'll get going."

Jinny went outside to a barren stretch of waste ground at the side of the sale ground. Here the worst of the ponies and horses were standing, tethered to rails. She walked between the rows of animals, her feelings numbed by what she saw. Rheumy, dull eyes were half hidden under drooping eyelids, worn out heads hung down from slack necks, brittle stick legs supported ridged ribs and jutting hip bones. Many were galled or scarred. Hardly any of them had the energy left to look round when Jinny passed them.

She forced herself to walk along the rows of horses until she had seen them all. Neither Shantih nor Bramble were there.

Jinny went back to the covered part of the sale ground and once more went round the horses that were tied to the wall. Already there were gaps where horses had been bought and taken away. It was already possible that Shantih had been there and they had missed her.

Jinny wached at the ringside from two until three. Halfway through her hour, Ken joined her.

"Why must they hit them?" he asked, as yet another pony was chased round the ring to the accompaniment of the auctioneer's patter.

"Makes them look lively," said Jinny bitterly.

She was watching a nappy chestnut pony being ridden round the ring by a scared child, when Ken touched her arm.

"That one," he said, and drew her attention to a black pony that was next but one to come into the ring.

The pony had a hogged mane, clipped heels and a ridiculously short tail. His face had a white blaze and he had four white socks above his blue-black hooves.

"I'll get the police," said Ken. "Stop them going into the ring if you have to."

"Why?" Jinny asked, but Ken had gone.

Jinny walked over to the black pony. Ken couldn't possibly have thought it was Bramble. The pony looked almost a hand higher than Bramble. Bramble's neck was thick, short-set, and his head far heavier than this pony's. Then the pony turned round and looked at Jinny. She knew him at once. It was Bramble.

Jinny threw her arms round his neck, ran her hand over his withers and down his strong, square back. Touching him, she knew immediately that it really was Bramble. If Jinny had been blind she would have known him.

"Here, enough of that," said the man who was with Bramble.

Jinny scowled at him, wondering if he had stolen the ponies, had stolen Shantih.

"He's such a super pony," Jinny said, remembering that she had to stop them going into the ring. She ran Bramble's ears through her hands and felt the nick on the inside of his right one.

"Give over," said the man, pushing Jinny away.

"I'm only looking at him," said Jinny, in a Clare Burnley voice. "I do think he is such a super pony."

The auctioneer's hammer knocked down the chestnut pony. The scared child, wiping her eyes on the sleeve of her jacket, was led out of the ring and a piebald pony was led in. Bramble was next.

"I think he's absolutely what we are looking for," said Jinny. "I know mummy will just love him."

"Well, let your mum bid for him when I take him into the ring. You clear off."

"Do you need to take him into the ring?" said Jinny, searching desperately for any sign of Ken returning with

99

the police. "I know we'll want to have him. He is just what we've been looking for. Can't you wait here and we'll buy him from you? Whatever price you like."

"You barmy or what?" said the man, glaring suspiciously at Jinny as the bidding for the piebald rose steadily.

The piebald was sold and still there was no sign of Ken.

"You can't," said Jinny. "You can't take him into the ring." But already the piebald was out of the ring and the man was leading Bramble in.

"No!" cried Jinny. "Stop!" But the man strode past her and the auctioneer started the bidding.

Jinny stared round the sale ring. There was still no sign of the policemen, Miss Tuke, Sue or Ken. Cupping her hands round her mouth, Jinny bellowed their names.

"Quickly! Come quickly!" she roared. "Bramble's in the ring."

Then she dashed across the ring to the foot of the auctioneer's stand.

"That's one of them," she said, shouting up at the auctioneer. "One of the stolen ponies we told you about. He can't sell it. It doesn't belong to him. Ken's gone for the police."

From the tiered seats around the sale ring, people began to stand up to get a better view of the disturbance, their voices rising in a buzz of curiosity.

The man leading Bramble told Jinny to get out or he'd get the police to her.

"You saw me this morning," Jinny shouted at the auctioneer. "I'm with Miss Tuke."

The auctioneer looked down at Jinny with obvious disapproval. For a moment she thought that he too was going to tell her to go away, but then, to her relief, two of the policemen came running into the ring. One spoke to the man with Bramble and took him out of the ring, the other explained what was happening to the auctioneer.

"He wouldn't listen to me," Jinny said, as she hurried over to where Miss Tuke was being loud and definite.

"Utterly positive," she was saying. "Bred him myself. That's my mark on his ear. All that white they've daubed over him—that'll come off. Daresay a good shower of rain would shift the lot."

To Jinny's dismay, the man with Bramble swore that he knew nothing about him. He said he was a cattle dealer and he had only brought Bramble in to the sale as a favour to a friend of his.

"Chap called Vernon, Sid Vernon. Dealer he is. Deals in anything. Told me the pony belonged to a kid and he wanted it selling, quiet like, so there'd be no fuss with the kid. He's done a few favours for me, on and off like. Wasn't doing anything special today myself so I said I'd oblige and bring the pony in for him. Don't know more than that. You check up on him."

"Might be just what we had in mind, a little checking up," said one of the policemen.

"Three of them," said Miss Tuke with satisfaction, when the policemen had got all the details they needed from her and one of them had gone with the man to Sid Vernon's yard. "But no nearer to getting to the bottom of all this—finding out who is responsible for it."

"Would you have known Bramble?" Sue asked.

When they had examined Bramble carefully they had found black roots on all his white parts, where they had been bleached.

"Known him anywhere," said Miss Tuke.

"I would never have known him," declared Sue.

Jinny said nothing. Once Ken had pointed Bramble out to her then she had known him, but not before. Earlier in the morning she must have passed him and not recognised him. "But I would know Shantih," she thought. "No matter what they've done to her, I would know her."

"Where is she?" Jinny whispered to Bramble. "What have they done to her?"

It was late afternoon before the policeman came to tell Miss Tuke that there had been no one at Sid Vernon's yard.

"Drew a blank at his house as well. Next-door neighbour said he is away a lot. But we'll get him. From the looks of his yard, I'd say he's only a middleman. We'll find out though. We're keeping the other man for questioning."

By five o'clock there were only a few animals left. The last of the bidding was over, the seats round the ring empty.

Jinny walked intently round the sale ground, moving from one horse to the next, ignoring the empty rings hanging from the walls and the empty pens. Only a few hours ago they had been full of life. The whole sale ground had been filled with men and animals, loud with voices and the ring of hooves. Now it was almost silent. A few hours ago, Jinny had been filled with hope that she would find Shantih, that by now they would have been driving home to Finmory, and by tomorrow Shantih would have been back in her own field.

Why had they found the ponies and not Shantih? Why had Shantih not been at the sale? Or had she been there and Jinny hadn't recognised her? Seen her and hadn't known her? Or had missed her? Had Shantih been one of the horses that had been taken from one box into another? Had she never been brought into the sale?

Jinny was almost running now. So clearly in her mind's eye she could see the flat curve of Shantih's cheek, the flare of her nostrils, the shell curve of her ears, and her dark eyes watching for her mistress.

"Shantih," Jinny called silently. "Shantih." And clearly in her mind's ear was the sound of Shantih's answering whinny.

Conspicuous now that the sale ground was nearly empty, Jinny dashed to and fro between the few horses that were left; avoiding Miss Tuke, Ken and Sue; refusing to admit that Shantih was not there; refusing to start on the night journey back to Finmory without her horse.

Miss Tuke appeared, marching between the pens towards Jinny.

"Well, that's that," she said, pouncing on Jinny. "Got to get back. Three out of four. Pretty good. At least you've got Bramble back."

Jinny couldn't speak. It wasn't possible. Not possible that they hadn't found Shantih.

"Right then. Off we go," said Miss Tuke.

CHAPTER ELEVEN

They drove through the city, then through the red-brick suburbs where dual carriageway changed into motorway. The wheels of the box purred along the road to the north.

Miss Tuke and Sue discussed the sale. Ken sat silently while Kelly slept with his head on Ken's knee. Behind them the three ponies shifted their weight to keep their balance as the box swung round corners.

Jinny sat staring through the cab window, seeing nothing, hearing nothing. Things had no names, were strangely flat and distant. Her touch carried no messages to her brain. There was nothing but a metal pain. The moment when the dentist's drill touched the nerve in her tooth, the flash second of unendurable agony, was locked hard and heavy and constant in her head and chest.

"Shantih! Shantih! Shantih!"

Jinny gritted her teeth to lock in the sound. If it escaped she wouldn't be able to stop the scream going on and on, wiping her out.

"Don't know about you lot," said Miss Tuke, "but I could do with a good meal, something you can get a knife and fork into. Utter disgrace having no decent catering at a place the size of that sale ground. We'll stop at the first service point."

"They're very expensive, motorway stops," said Sue doubtfully. "Dad says they're daylight robbery."

"On me," said Miss Tuke. "Left to myself, I'd still have been chasing the tinkers round Alec's farm."

"In that case, I'm starving," agreed Sue.

"What about Ken?" asked Miss Tuke. "Chips? Baked beans?"

"Miss Tuke's going to buy us a meal," Sue told Ken. "Will you have chips and baked beans?"

Ken showed no sign of having heard her. They turned off the motorway and drove into the car park at the side of the service station. Glass doors opened on to a brilliantly-lit hall, a self-service shop dazzled under neon lighting, teenage boys played slot machines and, at the far end of the hallway, concrete stairs led up to a cafeteria.

"Everybody out," said Miss Tuke.

"For lady you walk through hell," said Ken, as the glass doors opened in front of them and they drowned in the electric glare.

Jinny followed them in. If she had stayed alone in the horsebox she would have started to cry, and she couldn't do that until she was alone at Finmory.

They climbed the stairs and walked along a glass and concrete tube that crossed the motorway. It lay beneath them, a ribbon of light, constant movement that appeared to be motionless.

The self-service cafeteria was neon-lit and plastic. The tables, chairs and floor were plastic. Ranged along a metal and plastic counter were plates of food sealed over with polythene. Even the people were plastics—the night travellers, grey plastic; the waitresses who hovered behind the counter waiting to replace the plates of plastic food, were made of shiny pink and white plastic.

Miss Tuke and Sue filled their trays with food, Jinny took two egg sandwiches wrapped in polythene and Ken an apple.

"Take the seeds home and plant them. A real orchard springing up from a place like this," he said, not eating it but putting it in his pocket.

Jinny took one bite of her sandwich, chewed on the mixture of tough egg, yellow grease and cotton-wool bread. She left the rest. Miss Tuke and Sue started on their tomato soup, telling each other how hungry they were.

Suddenly Ken sprang up, angular, long-haired. He leapt through the cafeteria, out through the glass doors, and danced his way along the glass tunnel in a weird silhouette of freedom.

"Where's he off to now?" demanded Miss Tuke, while Sue stared in shocked disbelief at such behaviour.

"Fresh air," said Jinny. "He can't breathe in a place like this."

"He is unbalanced," judged Miss Tuke. "If he were a horse I'd have him shot."

Jinny waited until Miss Tuke and Sue had started on their fish and chips, then she made an excuse and went to find Ken.

She searched through the complex but could see no sign of him. Only ghost people like herself wandered in this garish wilderness. She passed a young woman crying in an older man's arms, a screaming toddler being orbited along by his running mother, a boy with a blank, stoned face sitting staring at his own hand.

"Maybe they are all like me," Jinny thought. "All the people who are here are here because something dreadful has happened to them."

She went out into the dark.

"You will never see Shantih again. Never," she told herself. Having had Ken with them had made no difference. Bramble would be back in his field tomorrow, but not Shantih. Never, ever again would she look out of her bedroom window, call "Shantih" and hear her horse's answering whinny.

"Don't cry," Jinny told herself. "Not yet. Don't start."

Ken materialised at her side. Kelly pushed his wet nose against her hand. They walked together through the car park, past the towering bulk of container lorries and tankers, trucks and cars.

"We are their prey," said Ken. "They've captured us and brought us here. While we are inside, the electricity sucks life from us," and he leapt in karate chops against the cars and lorries.

From one of the parked floats came the sound of cattle. For an instant, Jinny didn't realise what the noise meant. She only thought of it as a farm noise, a comforting, country sound. Then she felt Ken stiffen, and realised that they

105

were cattle being taken to market, or already sold and on their way to the slaughterhouse.

Jinny shuddered and turned quickly away, not looking at the float.

"No you don't," said Ken. He caught her by the arm and forced her to turn round. "You made me come to the sale, so now you look. See what I see," he said, as Jinny struggled to escape from him, run to the other end of the car park and shut herself away in Miss Tuke's box.

The float was packed with calves. Through the open slats Jinny saw their dark eyes, doe-gentle, liquid, reflecting neon light, glistening muzzles and moving shadows cast by their bat ears.

"They are so beautiful," said Ken. "Each one perfect and this is what we do to them."

"Let me go," cried Jinny, but Ken ignored her.

"Breathe with love," he said. "Give them your silence. Let them know that there are humans who care." And he forced Jinny to stand silently, to be aware.

As Jinny stood there, it did seem that the calves knew they were there, as if they shared some dim understanding.

"They do know," said Ken at last. "We know when a God gives his attention to us; that moment, that inkling. We all know what it feels like. In the East, they know by the scent which God holds them in its hands."

Somewhere in the parking space a horse whinnied.

"Shantih!" screamed Jinny, and immediately she had broken from Ken's hold and was running through the rows of vehicles, shouting her horse's name at the top of her voice. "Shantih! Shantih!"

The whinnying that answered her was as frantic and desperate as Jinny's own voice.

"There," cried Jinny. "There. She's in that horsebox. We've found her. Shantih! Shantih!"

"You're certain it is her?" asked Ken.

"Totally positive. I'd know her whinny anywhere. It couldn't be any other horse. If there were a million other horses I'd know it was Shantih."

For a moment they both stood staring up at the box.

"Come on," said Jinny. "We've got to get in to her. Quick, before anyone comes."

The back of the horsebox was securely padlocked. Jinny sped round to the cabin. The passenger door was locked. Desperately she ran round to the driver's door. The metal handle moved beneath her hand. The unlocked door opened. Jinny scrambled inside. She saw a door at the back of the cabin and opened it with shaking hands.

For a second she stood, unable to move, hardly able to trust her eyes.

"Shantih!" she screamed, and in the instant had squeezed her way into the back of the box, to where Shantih was standing, tied to a rail at the side.

Jinny flung her arms round Shantih's neck and buried her face against her mane; tears poured down her face and her breath sobbed out of her body. She had found her horse, had broken free of the nightmare. It had not happened. It was not true.

Jinny ran her hands over Shantih's neck and head, felt her soft muzzle lipping against her cheek; her forelock and mane slipped like silk between Jinny's fingers. Quickly she checked over Shantih's legs and quarters, making certain that Shantih had not been harmed in any way. At the last minute of the eleventh hour the horror of losing Shantih had let her go.

"Is it her?" Ken asked from outside.

His voice brought Jinny back to the present and she scrambled out of the box.

"Yes," she told him. "We've got to get her out before the thieves come back." She looked hurriedly over her shoulder for any sign of the owners of the horsebox.

"Can't get her out," Ken said, "unless we've keys for the padlocks. Better get Miss Tuke."

"You go," said Jinny. "I'll stay here."

"Right," said Ken, and raced off into the darkness.

Left alone, Jinny felt suddenly vulnerable and afraid. If the horse thieves came back now she didn't know what she could do to stop them driving away. A sudden vivid picture flashed through her mind of the horsebox with Shantih

107

inside it being driven away, while she stood helplessly watching it go.

"I've got to get inside with Shantih," Jinny thought. "If Ken gets back first with Sue and Miss Tuke I'll hear them, but if it's the horse thieves, at least I'll be with Shantih."

Jinny climbed into the cabin and then into the back of the box, carefully shutting all the doors behind her.

Shantih whickered a welcome, stretching out her head to breathe over Jinny.

"Where have you been?" Jinny whispered to her. "What did they do to you?" She stood waiting, one arm over Shantih's withers, her ears peeled for the sound of Ken bringing Miss Tuke and Sue.

"Perhaps they're phoning the police," Jinny thought, as each minute stretched out endlessly and still they did not come. "Oh, hurry, hurry. We've got to get out of here before they catch us."

The sound of footsteps came out of the darkness. Relief flooded over Jinny. It must be Ken, Miss Tuke and Sue. She waited, poised, listening for just another moment before she burst out of the box to join them; to tell Sue how she had heard Shantih; to listen to Miss Tuke's bossy efficiency taking charge of the rescue.

The footsteps drew nearer, but they were not Ken's slow stride, Miss Tuke's bustling or Sue's light step. They were strong and heavy and unknown. Biting her knuckles, Jinny waited, praying they would pass the horsebox and go on to another car or van.

She heard men's low, angry voices as they strode up to the box and climbed in.

Frantically, Jinny looked for somewhere to hide, but there was nowhere; no pile of straw or heap of rugs. She pressed herself against the back of the box where she would be hidden by the door opening from the cabin. If they only looked through the door at Shantih, there was a chance that she might not be noticed, but if one of the men came into the back of the box they were bound to see her.

The box started with a jerk as the driver swung out of the car park and on to the motorway. Standing in the darkness, Jinny could hear the sound of the men's voices. One seemed an older man with a deep sarcastic voice, while the other man, who was driving the float, sounded younger.

Now and again Jinny caught snatches of their conversation. The older man seemed to be the boss. He was called Major Fitzsimmons and obviously employed the younger man.

"All right for you," Jinny heard the younger man saying. "You're blooming calm you are, Major blooming Fitzsimmons. Picking up her ladyship and then stopping for a meal. You're O.K., you are." Then the words were lost in the crash and rattle of the horsebox.

"How do you know that Sid Vernon hasn't spilt the beans?" Jinny heard the young man demanding.

"Because, just like you, my dear boy, Sid doesn't know any beans worth spilling."

Straining her ears, Jinny tried to follow the conversation, but again the words were drowned by the noise of the box.

They seemed to have been driving for about half an hour when Jinny heard the older man beginning to open the door into the back of the box.

"I'll take a look at her," he was saying.

There was nothing Jinny could do. Only stand frozen, waiting.

The door opened, a man's head peered in at Shantih.

"Bright as the proverbial button," he said, shutting the door again, while Jinny's heart banged so loudly she was sure they must hear it in the cabin.

Suddenly Jinny heard the sound of a police siren growing louder and louder as a car scorched towards them.

"Lord, the blooming cops," swore the young man, and Jinny felt the box surge forward. The sudden movement threw her into a corner and made Shantih stagger and plunge to keep her balance.

"Slow down, you fool. What do you want them to think? That we've something to hide? They'll have us for speeding if you go on like that."

The police car drew level with the box, kept pace with it, its siren banshee above the traffic.

"Do what they want," Jinny heard the older man say. His voice without its edge of mockery was cold and rasping. "They've no evidence. Horse belongs to my daughter. Leave it to me. You're a hired driver, know nothing."

"I blooming told you we should have scarpered the minute they picked up the first two ponies," the young man muttered, as Jinny felt the box being driven on to the hard shoulder of the motorway and jammed to a halt.

She heard the police car scream in in front of them, its doors being opened and running footsteps race to the box. Holding her breath, she listened, hardly able to believe that the police had found them.

"Good evening, sir," said an official voice, as the door was opened. "Can we trouble you to take a look in the back? Reason to believe that you may be carrying something of interest to us."

"Good evening, officer," said the older man. "Rather a sudden demand. Got my daughter's horse in the back. If that's of interest to you, in you come."

Jinny heard the man jump out, the policeman climb into the cab and open the door. In a shaft of light, a helmeted head looked in at her.

Jinny stood with her arm round Shantih, opening and shutting her mouth, unable to think of a word to say. She was held in the policeman's torch like a rabbit in headlights. There was nothing in her mind but the incredible, dazed delight of the fact that now Shantih was truly safe.

The police contacted their station, where Miss Tuke, Ken and Sue had all been waiting. They arrived in the horsebox and Shantih was transferred to it. The two men were taken away for questioning.

"We thought we'd lost you too," Sue told Jinny, "when we got out to the car park and found the box had gone. Ken guessed that you must have gone with Shantih, so Miss Tuke rushed us off to the nearest police station. Ken had the number of the horsebox and the police did the rest. Whatever would you have done if we hadn't found you?"

"Dunno," said Jinny. "Hadn't thought. It didn't matter. All that mattered was that I'd found Shantih."

Back in the police station, Jinny told the policemen what she had overheard, showed them the description of Shantih signed by the vet and listened to Miss Tuke being loud and efficient. Jinny floated on a dream of delirious happiness. Shantih was safe.

"We've to thank you for tonight's work," the policeman said, as he came with them to the door of the station. "We've been on the lookout for Major Fitzsimmons, as he calls himself, for some time. We knew there was one man behind the horse thefts but we couldn't pin him down. Didn't want to bring in the little men until we'd got the brain behind them. Now, thanks to you, we've got him."

Jinny insisted on travelling in the back with Shantih. She stood leaning against the sides of the box, feeling Shantih's warm breath on her face, twisting strands of Shantih's mane between her fingers. The box rumbled into life, the ponies propping themselves on outstretched forelegs as Miss Tuke drove on to the motorway.

"Home," said Jinny, happiness bubbling in her. "Back to Finmory."

They had phoned Mr. and Mrs. Manders to let them know what had happened, and the lights were on in Finmory House as they drove up the drive. Jinny's parents and Mike were waiting at the door to welcome them.

Stiff-legged, Jinny stomped down the ramp, Shantih clattering at her side and jumping from the ramp with an enormous leap that almost dragged the halter from Jinny's grasp.

"Beyond me what you wanted her back for," said Mike, "the mad idiot," while Sue and Miss Tuke told them the details of their day.

Sue led Bramble and Jinny took Shantih, down through the garden to their field. In front of her, Jinny could just make out the bulk of Bramble, could just hear Sue chatting to him. The darkness was velvet soft about Jinny. From the shore she could make out the soft sighing of the sea. She sprang up on to Shantih's back and rode the last few steps to the field.

"I should have died if I hadn't found her," Jinny said,

leaning on the familiar field gate as Shantih thudded round the field.

"You wouldn't," said Sue.

"A bit of me would have," said Jinny. "Truly. A bit of my heart would have been torn out."

When they got back to the house, Miss Tuke was climbing into the cabin of her box.

"You're not going so soon?" shouted Jinny, who had been thinking of coffee and food, to be eaten slowly as they sat round the kitchen table reliving the day.

"Must. Trekking tomorrow. No peace for the wicked." Miss Tuke slammed the cabin door and switched on the engine.

"Thank you for everything," Jinny shouted. "Thank you."

"My pleasure," said Miss Tuke, thinking of tomorrow's trek. Then she suddenly stuck her head out of the cab window. "How are you getting to Inverburgh?" she asked.

"To where?" said Jinny, trying to think why Miss Tuke thought she wanted to go to Inverburgh.

"Saturday. The show. I'll phone you tomorrow night. See if you want a lift."

"But I can't take Shantih to the show," said Jinny. "Not after I've just rescued her."

"Why not? Day's rest tomorrow. Do her no harm."

Jinny stared up vacantly at Miss Tuke. It seemed like years since she had given a thought to Inverburgh Show.

"Can't let Clare Burnley win all the cups," laughed Miss Tuke, as she drove away.

CHAPTER TWELVE

The dew lay thickly on grass and hedgerows, diamonding spiders' webs, creating crystal palaces from last year's bracken. Jinny left a trail of dark footprints as she walked down to the horses' field in the early morning. She walked slowly, knowing there was no need to hurry, Shantih and Bramble were safe. Already she had seen them from her bedroom window, floating shapes in the morning mists.

Jinny climbed into the field and stood waiting as Shantih walked towards her, precise and delicate. The Arab's white stockings were darkened with dew, her ears listening for the sound of Jinny's voice, her nostrils trembling a welcome, her eyes under their long lashes glistened dark-silver. Jinny held out her hand and Shantih lipped gently over her palm. Finding nothing, she lifted her head, whiffled at Jinny's neck, tickling her ear.

Bramble, suspecting food, came trotting up. He still looked strangely shorn, and, despite herself, Jinny couldn't help smiling at the difference it had made to him.

"Wonder if you'll be able to jump any better without all that hair?" Jinny asked him, producing sugar lumps from her anorak pocket and giving them to Bramble and Shantih.

"Hi," said Ken, stopping on his way to the shore. "Settled in again?"

"If you hadn't come, we wouldn't have found Shantih," said Jinny.

The knowledge that Shantih was safely back in her field dazzled the whole of Jinny's being. She didn't know of anything that would have been enough to express the way she felt.

"If Miss Tuke and Sue hadn't been hungry we wouldn't have stopped at all," Ken said.

113

"But if you hadn't made me look at the calves I would have been back in Miss Tuke's box. I would never have heard Shantih from there. So nearly, nearly I would never have seen her again," Jinny said. "It was so lucky that she was there in the car park. Such a coincidence. Even now I can hardly believe it."

"Coincidence!" said Ken scornfully. "There's no such thing. It's a cover-up word for a chain reaction, a linking of incidents which we hardly understand. We're only beginning to be aware of them."

"What links brought Shantih to the car park?"

"Your love for her," said Ken slowly. "The tinker boy's courage. Me coming to the sale instead of chickening out? The calves? The men in the horsebox? Who knows? These and a billion more subtleties create what we call co-incidence." He laughed, harsh and sudden. "We know nothing," he said, and, running his hand over Shantih's neck, he went on down to the sea.

"And what are you going to do today?" said Mrs. Manders, when the breakfast dishes had been washed up and put away.

"Lie in the sun," said Jinny. "I'm going to lie in Shantih's field and watch her. I might, just might, draw her as well."

"Hardly *Homes and Gardens'* idea of the ideal hostess," said Mrs. Manders. "What about Sue?"

"I shall sleep," said Sue. "Lie in Shantih's field and sleep."

"And there's Ewan MacKenzie's ponies. Have you to ride them back?"

"Not today," said Jinny. "We will, but not today."

Although Jinny took her drawing pad and pencils with her, her attempts at drawing soon changed into lying back with Sue, watching the horses grazing.

"If I want to," Jinny thought, "I can get up and walk across the field and Shantih is there. Really there."

To prove it to herself, she got up and walked across to Shantih to clap her neck, run her hand under her mane and sprawl over her back.

"Ten times this morning," said Sue's drowsy voice. "Ten times you've had to make sure that she isn't a mirage."

Jinny sat back down, resting her chin on her knees.

"Why do you think they stole them?"

"For money," said Sue. "Pretty easy money. We wouldn't have had a chance of tracing them if we hadn't found the *Horse and Hound*."

"And I would never have found it if Tam hadn't told us about the horses being at the Barony."

"I'd say he deserves a V.C. for coming to tell us. Jake would have killed him if he'd found out."

In the afternoon they rode bareback down to the shore. Everything that Jinny had taken for granted before Shantih was stolen was now shimmering with delight. Even putting on Shantih's halter was like some joyous miracle, some special gift from the gods, a touch of heaven.

When they reached the sands, the contentment was still there. It was enough to sit on the rocks holding Shantih and Bramble and stare out to sea.

"If only they could tell us where they've been," Sue said, as they rode back to Finmory.

"One thing, Shantih didn't do any work while she was away," laughed Jinny.

She was riding Shantih in a halter and the Arab was flirting from side to side, gravel spurting from her hooves as she kicked and shied, desperate to gallop.

They had just got back to the stables and were brushing down their horses when Mike came looking for Jinny.

"Phone," he said.

"Miss Tuke?" Jinny asked, thinking it was too early for Miss Tuke's evening call.

"Don't know. Mum answered it. She didn't say who it was."

Tipping oats and nuts into Shantih's trough, Jinny left her and went in to the phone.

"Hullo," she said.

"Hello," said Clare Burnley's voice.

"Puke, double puke," thought Jinny, as Clare's loud insincerity gushed into her ear, telling Jinny how utterly delighted they had all been to hear that she had found Shantih.

Jinny held the phone at arm's length, and, in a few minutes, Clare told her that she must fly.

"Right," said Jinny. "Do that."

"One more thing. Are you going to the show tomorrow?"

"Why?"

"I was only wondering. I mean to say, one does know how keen you are, and trying so hard with your jumping on that totally unsuitable beast. One was wondering."

"Was one," said Jinny.

"Or are you chickening out? Must fly. Bye." And Clare put the phone down.

"Well!" exclaimed Jinny. "Of all the cheek!"

"Who was it?" asked her mother.

"Clare Burnley," said Jinny. "Phoning me! Wanting to know if I'm going in for the jumping at the show."

"Are you?"

"Don't know whether it would be fair to Shantih, although she seems fresh enough."

Miss Tuke phoned in the evening. She had heard from the police that Major Fitzsimmons had been the man they were after.

"He worked through middlemen," Miss Tuke told Jinny. "Like Fred the driver, or Sid Vernon. Jake had nothing much to do with it. Only showed them where they could leave the stolen horses while they were up here. Still, he knew what was going on."

"Why wasn't Shantih at the sale?" Jinny demanded.

"Special order, you might say. They'd left her somewhere for the day. Picked her up after the sale and were taking her to their customer. A friend of the Major's. That's why he was there. He normally left the delivery to the others. The police told me to congratulate you on tracking him down. Seems he was the mastermind behind it all. They're both being charged. I've to go down to give evidence. See if we can get them behind bars. That'll stop them causing any more trouble."

At Miss Tuke's words, Jinny saw the men crouching in

116

a rat-trap cage, tearing at the bars, fighting to escape. She pushed the thought away. Jinny didn't want them to come back stealing horses but she didn't want to think of them shut up in prison. She wanted them to feel the way she had done all day, when everything was alive with joy. Every least thing sparkling and unique. If they felt like that they wouldn't want to steal.

"Are you still there?" demanded Miss Tuke.

"Yes. Oh, er, yes," said Jinny, coming back to earth.

"Then listen. I said, 'Are you coming to Inverburgh?'"

"Well . . ." said Jinny.

"Your horse is quite fit. I can only take Shantih. Haven't room for Bramble. What do you say? Pick you up to-morrow morning? Eightish?"

"Well . . ." said Jinny again. She had so totally forgotten the world of show jumping and shows and cups. It was enough to have Shantih. She didn't need any more.

"Brisk up," said Miss Tuke. "I can imagine the state you're in. Come to the show. Give that Clare Burnley a run for her money."

At the mention of Clare Burnley's name, Jinny felt the thrill of competition shiver through her. To go to Inverburgh Show and beat Clare Burnley. Perhaps Shantih would behave herself tomorrow. Perhaps tomorrow would be the day when Shantih would jump in the ring the way she did at home. For weeks Jinny had been preparing for Inverburgh Show. Suddenly it seemed a pity not to go. She would be sorry tomorrow if she decided to stay at home.

"Be ready for eight," said Miss Tuke, and put the phone down.

CHAPTER THIRTEEN

Shantih, groomed to perfection, stood at Finmory's front door waiting for Miss Tuke to arrive. Jinny, holding her, was dressed in jodhpurs and jacket, white shirt, tie and hard hat.

Yesterday evening had turned into a frantic preparation for Inverburgh Show—Mrs. Manders pressing Jinny's riding clothes, Jinny grooming Shantih and Sue cleaning her tack.

Sue had said she would enjoy going to a show without a horse, having a chance to look round without worrying about what Pippen was doing.

"Anyway," she'd said, "it wouldn't be fair, exposing Bramble to the public gaze in his shorn condition."

Miss Tuke's box drove into the yard.

"Get her loaded," called Miss Tuke. "Highland Ponies in Hand is the second class. Mustn't be late."

Two lady trekkers, who were entering Miss Tuke's Highlands for the Handy Horse, climbed down from the cabin and came to help. Miss Tuke had three Highlands in the box, all spruced and gleaming, hooves oiled and manes brushed out into clouds of hair. They strained against their halters, trying to see what was happening outside.

"Jinny, travel in the back with Shantih. Rather crushed in the front," said Miss Tuke.

So Jinny stayed with Shantih, watching the ramp swing up, blocking out the light.

"A day at Inverburgh Show," thought Jinny. "A day with Shantih." And it didn't matter, didn't matter in the least, how Shantih behaved. Jinny couldn't have cared less whether she won anything or not. Enough to be there, being driven to the show with Shantih.

Jinny felt the box stop at the gate of the show field. She heard Miss Tuke speaking to the men at the gate and then the box drove on, lurching over the grass until it came to a shuddering halt. The Highlands, knowing they had arrived, kicked impatiently, wanting to be let out.

"Give over," roared Miss Tuke, as the ramp swung down, revealing white tents and marquees.

Jinny ran, light-footed, down the ramp at Shantih's side. The show field was already bustling with humans and animals. The smell of trodden grass pricked in Jinny's nostrils and she stared round at Persil-white sheep, cattle scrubbed and polished, carthorses primped out with ribbons. Children on shaggy ponies cantered about, their faces serious under hard hats. A few adults rode show horses, red-faced farmers leant against the sides of their cattle floats, talking to friends they hadn't seen since the last Inverburgh Show. Jinny grinned to herself, remembering last year when she had come to the show with the Burnleys.

Sue was helping Miss Tuke with the Highlands, so Jinny mounted and began to ride round on Shantih. She had decided only to enter for the Open Jumping and that wasn't until the afternoon. Jinny relaxed, enjoying herself. As she rode about, people she hardly knew came up to speak to her, telling her how pleased they were that she had got Shantih back. Jinny nodded, smiling, saying, Yes, yes, yes she had been lucky, and feeling as if she would burst for happiness, for joy to be riding there on Shantih.

"And none the worse she's looking for her wee adventure," said Mr. MacKenzie, coming up to speak to Jinny with his cloned grandson in his arms.

"Och, but I'm pleased you were finding her. It's your madness I'd have been missing if she'd been for the sausages."

Miss Tuke's Highlands were placed first and second. Miss Tuke was chuffed.

"Did *not* expect it," she said, pinning the rosettes on her windscreen.

"Jolly well done! Congrats!" shouted Clare Burnley, as

she rode past on Jasper, looking as if she was about to show a horse at Wembley.

"Thanks," said Miss Tuke. "Pleased myself."

"Terribly sweet grey that won it," said Clare. "One was wondering if it might not be rather fun to buy a Highland down south, bring it up here and see how it would show."

"Really," said Miss Tuke, as Clare rode on. "She is an impossible girl."

Watching Clare riding into the ring for the Over 14.2 showing class, Jinny wholeheartedly agreed with Miss Tuke. Jasper, her black thoroughbred, was so obviously superior to any of the other show horses.

"To bring them all the way from Sussex!" declared Jinny in disgust.

"Just a minute," said Miss Tuke, who was standing by Jinny's side. "What have we here?"

Into the ring rode a lady on a bay horse.

"Mrs. Bowen," said Miss Tuke. "They've bought a bung. not far from us. Knew she was horsy, but not this!"

The bay the woman was riding was about seventeen hands high. He strode into the ring with an assured presence, arching his neck and trotting out with a bold courage. Beside this majesty, Jasper seemed to dwindle into little more than a blood weed. His thoroughbred head was waspish, his hocks weak and his shoulders too straight.

Clare scowled at the woman, drew Jasper together, and, when they were asked to trot, sent him on at a showy extended pace. Jinny had always thought that Clare looked better on Huston. She was too heavy for Jasper, took the light out of him. With a more sympathetic rider he might have lifted, shown his qualities of air and flame, but with Clare on top he began to resist, switching his tail, crabbing and dropping behind the bit.

"This could be it," said Miss Tuke, and she was right. The judge put the bay first, Jasper second. Clare had not won the cup.

"First time for years," said Miss Tuke, tucking in her lips, lifting her eyebrows, twinkling at Jinny out of the corner of her eyes.

With a face as sullen as late November, Clare followed Mrs. Bowen round the ring.

Mike and Mrs. Manders arrived at lunchtime, bringing a picnic basket.

"Have you done your thing yet?" Mike asked.

"This afternoon," Jinny said. "Open Jumping. There is only one show jumping class this year."

"Always used to be two," stated Miss Tuke.

"They've made the other one for ponies of 14.2 and Under. So I could only have gone in for one jumping class anyway."

"That means," said Miss Tuke, "that Clare only has one more chance to win a cup."

"She'll win it," said Jinny, not caring, as she looked up from where she lay stretched out on the grass, holding Shantih's reins, gazing at the threatening bulk of Shantih's head descending from above, wanting a bit of her cake. "She always does."

"Always *did* win the showing," said Miss Tuke.

Moira Wilson on Snuff won the 14.2 and Under jumping class with a clear round. A boy on a bay pony was second with one refusal for three faults, and a tall, spotty girl was third. Her flea-bitten grey had the pole off the second jump for four faults. Jinny, who had been riding Shantih in, came back just in time to see them cantering round the ring.

The jumps were put up for the Over 14.2 jumping class —the Open Jumping. The first jump up the side of the ring was an upright of red and white poles, followed by a stile and rails and a third jump of parallel poles. At the top of the ring there was a brush jump, then, diagonally across the ring, there was a double. Back up the opposite side of the ring there was a white gate and another brush fence with straw bales in front of it. Finally, down the centre of the ring there was a high wall of red and white bricks.

Jinny sat on Shantih, watching as a young farmer on a heavy bay rode the course. He had a pole down at the second part of the double, two refusals at the brush and bales and a brick out of the wall. He rode out, good-naturedly cursing his horse.

Last year, when Jinny had ridden in the Handy Horse, she had been tight with nerves as she had waited to ride into the ring, but today she wasn't in the least nervous. She was too glad to be riding Shantih; too glad that the nightmare of the horse sale was over, too glad that she had found Shantih, to care about her performance in the ring. She was looking forward to jumping; totally, completely looking forward to being allowed to jump.

Four more riders had rounds punctuated with knockdowns and refusals and then Clare Burnley rode into the ring. She cantered a slow circle, holding the grey, Huston, between the control of her hands, seat and legs. She was in total command. She jumped a clear round, placing Huston at every jump, telling him where to take off, gathering him back into hand whenever he landed.

"Who has been watching the Germans?" said Miss Tuke.

The next woman had two refusals at the white gate on a Highland cross, and then it was Jinny.

Shantih cantered into the ring. Jinny felt her gay and willing and laughed aloud for joy, was filled with overbrimming delight.

Over the first three jumps they went in clear, bounding arcs, and at the top of the ring Shantih came sweetly back to hand. They cantered to the brush, sailed effortlessly over it and cantered across the ring to the double. Shantih was jumping more calmly than she had ever done before, as if at last she had absorbed Jinny's schooling and it had become her own true nature. She touched down between the double and cleared the second part with inches to spare. Up the side of the field they went, red-gold in the spring sunlight. Gate and brush were behind them. Round the top of the ring, to sail over the wall and ride out with a clear round.

"You were clear!" shrieked Sue. "A clear round! She was super."

"Drugged," said Miss Tuke. "You realise there may be tests?"

Mike and Mrs. Manders were amazed.

Jinny jumped to the ground, hiding her uncontrollable

122

grin under the saddle flap as she loosened Shantih's girths.

"You see," Jinny said, "you never believe me when I keep telling you she is improving," and she clapped Shantih's neck, scratched her face and slipped her forelock through her fingers.

There were no more clear rounds.

"Only you and Clare for the jump-off," said Sue.

But even as she watched Clare riding into the ring, Jinny couldn't feel desperate to win; didn't need to win.

"Watch out," mouthed Miss Tuke, as Clare, riding a super, correct round, placed Huston at the brush and bales. "He's too slow to clear that spread."

Miss Tuke was right. To the groans of the spectators, the pole on top of the brush rolled off. Clare had four faults. Her face set, her mouth frozen, she rode out of the ring.

"Do it again and you've won the cup," Mike said to Jinny. "Go on, show them."

Filled with delight at having a second chance to go round the course, Jinny rode into the ring. She knew that Shantih could have jumped twice the height of these jumps, and, behaving the way she was today, Jinny knew she would go round clear a second time.

Jinny felt the rhythm of her horse flowing through her as, with pricked ears, bright eyes, Shantih bounded clear over the jumps. As they turned into the wall, Jinny let her gallop on, felt her gather herself and take wings to soar over it. They were round clear for a second time.

There was clapping and a red rosette; shaking the hand of a fur-coated lady who smelt of talcum powder as she handed the cup up to Jinny. Overcome, Jinny tried to hand it back to her.

"It's yours. Yours to keep for the year," laughed the woman. "Give us a gallop round."

The cup held awkwardly in one hand, Jinny turned Shantih to gallop her round the ring. As she did so, she caught a glimpse of Clare Burnley's defeated face.

"But I won," thought Jinny. "Shantih won it. We've won the cup."

Standing in her stirrups, Jinny held the cup above her

head, rode round the ring laughing, the sun glinting on the cup in the way she had always known it would, the red rosette fluttering on Shantih's bridle. As she rode triumphant, Jinny blocked out the knowledge that Clare had been almost crying.

The congratulations and the cup were icing on the day. It would have been enough to have known that Shantih had improved; the minutes in the ring when she had been totally at one with Shantih would have been enough.

Clare's blank, bereft face pushed itself into Jinny's consciousness, would not leave her alone.

"But it is mine. I won it," she told herself. "It's what I've always wanted—to win a cup."

"You wanted a cup, but you didn't want to beat anyone," mocked the voice in Jinny's head. "Clare needed that cup more than you. You've got Shantih back. You didn't need a cup."

"I hate her," thought Jinny, "I hate her." But she didn't, not any more, not after having seen her.

A movement at the edge of the field caught Jinny's eye. It was Tam, the tinker boy. Jinny galloped across to him.

"Don't go," she shouted, and jumped to the ground beside him. "I've to thank you. We didn't find the horses at Barony but we did get them back in the end, thanks to you coming to tell us that they'd been there."

"Aye," said the boy staring at his feet.

Jinny looked at his pinched, smeared face; his old clothes, shiny with greasy dirt; his bird bones under the man's jacket. She should have had something to give him, something with which to thank him properly.

"Will you be staying on at McGowan's farm?"

"Moving on tonight."

Jinny had only a few pence in her pocket. She couldn't offer that to him.

"Listen," she said. "If you hadn't told us about the horses, I'd never have found Shantih. I love her the way you love your dog."

For an instant the boy looked straight at Jinny. His eyes,

dark as Jake's, were flecked with golden lights and fringed with black lashes.

"You saved Zed for us," he muttered.

"Well, you saved Shantih," replied Jinny. "If there's anything I can ever do to help you at any time, you've only to come to Finmory House and ask. You know where it is?"

"Aye."

"I mean it. Honestly. For ever."

"Aye," said the boy again. Then, with the characteristic duck of his head and shoulders, he was running away from Jinny. In seconds she had lost sight of him in the crowd.

Jinny sat staring into space, her hand on the reins checking Shantih's restless movements. She thought of the tinker boy going back to Jake while she would go back to Finmory, to all the warmth and protection of her life there. She shuddered, goose over her grave. But there was nothing she could do to change things.

Pushing back her hair, Jinny rode over to Miss Tuke's box. She passed Clare standing by herself, holding Huston.

"Not much better being Clare," Jinny thought, as Clare ignored her, looking pointedly in the opposite direction.

The cup that only a week ago had mattered so much to Jinny was now only a lump of useless metal. Winning cups was Clare's thing, not Jinny's.

Jinny left the cup in the back of their car. Before, she had been planning to keep it in a special place in her bedroom, but now it didn't matter. Her mother could find a place for it and next year Clare could win it back. Jinny didn't need cups. She had Ken and her family and their life at Finmory. She had Bramble and Shantih.

Sue went home in the Manders' car. Miss Tuke dropped Jinny and Shantih in Glenbost.

Jinny stood watching the horsebox being driven out of sight. It was early evening and the day nestled like a bird in the palm of her hand.

"You are fabulous," she said to Shantih. The moments in the ring when Shantih had truly been the winged horse of Jinny's dreams, were still vivid in her mind.

For a little way she walked beside Shantih, her arm over

Shantih's withers. Then she mounted and rode over the moor, following a sheep track that would bring her to the hill behind Finmory.

Jinny was considering the possibility of cheese buns and chocolate peppermint ice cream, for it had been a special day and her mother knew they were her favourite food, when she saw Ken standing on the hillside above her, waving and pointing to the sky. Jinny stopped Shantih and stared upwards, shading her eyes.

High in the clear, evening air, two birds flew in spiralling ecstasy. "Not buzzards or eagles," thought Jinny, and then she knew they were ospreys. Although their nest had been destroyed last year, they had come back to Finmory.

Jinny gazed entranced as they rose and fell with effortless power, playing in air.

She watched them without moving until, with great flaps of their wings, they both swung down the sky in the direction of Loch Varrich. They would rebuild their nest. This time their eggs would hatch.

Ken was waiting for her.

"It's all . . ." Jinny said, meaning the miracle of having found Shantih, the ospreys coming back again, and somehow Tam and Jake, and even the suffering of the animals. "It's all so . . ."

"Yes, isn't it," said Ken.

'JINNY' BOOKS
by Patricia Leitch

FOR LOVE OF A HORSE
When Jinny Manders rescues Shantih, a chestnut Arab, from a cruel circus, her dream of owning a horse seems to come true. But Shantih escapes on to the moors.

A DEVIL TO RIDE
Shantih, safe at last, is inseparable from Jinny. But the Arab is impossible to ride.

THE SUMMER RIDERS
Jinny is furious when Marlene, a city girl, comes to stay. But when Marlene's brother gets into trouble with the police, only Jinny and Shantih can help him.

NIGHT OF THE RED HORSE
When archaeologists excavate an ancient site, Jinny and Shantih fall under the terrifying power of the Celtic 'Pony Folk'.

GALLOP TO THE HILLS
When Ken Dawson's dog, Kelly, is wrongly accused of killing sheep, Jinny is determined to save him. But will she be in time?

HORSE IN A MILLION
Jinny is heart-broken when Shantih disappears one night. Desperate to find her, Jinny begins a dangerous search.

THE MAGIC PONY
Jinny's life is full of problems when she rescues an aged white pony. But an ancient magic intervenes.

RIDE LIKE THE WIND
Finmory House is to be sold, and Jinny and Shantih must go back to the city. How can Jinny save the home she loves?

Armada

CAPTAIN ARMADA

HI KIDS! I'VE GOT THE POWER TO BRING YOU FUN, ADVENTURE, AND EXCITEMENT!

Here are just a few of the best-selling titles that Armada has to offer:

- ☐ **Ride Like the Wind** Patricia Leitch 95p
- ☐ **The Wind in the Willows** Kenneth Grahame £1.25
- ☐ **The Treasure Hunters** Enid Blyton 85p
- ☐ **The Viking Symbol Mystery** Franklin W. Dixon 95p
- ☐ **Biggles Hunts Big Game** Captain W. E. Johns 95p
- ☐ **The Hidden Staircase** Carolyn Keene 95p
- ☐ **The Ghost Town Treasure** Ann Sheldon 95p
- ☐ **Mill Green on Stage** Alison Prince 95p
- ☐ **The Mystery of Shark Reef** Alfred Hitchcock 95p
- ☐ **The Dukes of Hazzard: Gone Racin'** Eric Alter 95p
- ☐ **The Chalet School Fete** Elinor M. Brent-Dyer 95p

Armadas are available in bookshops and newsagents, but can also be ordered by post.

HOW TO ORDER
ARMADA BOOKS, Cash Sales Dept., GPO Box 29, Douglas, Isle of Man, British Isles. Please send purchase price of book plus postage, as follows:—

    1—4 Books . . . . 10p per copy
    5 Books or more . . . no further charge
    25 Books sent post free within U.K.

Overseas Customers: 12p per copy.

NAME (Block letters) _____

ADDRESS _____

_____

_____

While every effort is made to keep prices low, it is sometimes necessary to increase prices on short notice. Armada Books reserve the right to show new retail prices on covers which may differ from those previously advertised in the text or elsewhere.